"Leave m-me alone," Paula whimpered,
too weak and despairing to speak
in anything but a low and husky tone.

Still feebly trying to resist, she thrust her
hands against his chest, but they were caught
and, without the slightest effort on his part,
Ramon held them behind her back and
looked down into her face with an expression
of triumph that brought fury to her eyes.
"What are you going to do now?" he asked
with some amusement.

ANNE HAMPSON
has the same impetuous streak as her heroines.
It often lands her in the middle of a new
country, a new adventure—and a new book.
Her firsthand knowledge of her settings and her
lively characters have combined to delight her
readers throughout the world.

Dear Reader:

Silhouette Romances is an exciting new publishing venture. We will be presenting the very finest writers of contemporary romantic fiction as well as outstanding new talent in this field. It is our hope that our stories, our heroes and our heroines will give you, the reader, all you want from romantic fiction.

Also, *you* play an important part in our future plans for Silhouette Romances. We welcome any suggestions or comments on our books and I invite you to write to us at the address below.

So, enjoy this book and all the wonderful romances from Silhouette. They're for *you!*

Karen Solem
Editor-in-Chief
Silhouette Books
P.O. Box 769
New York, N.Y. 10019

ANNE HAMPSON
The Dawn Steals Softly

Silhouette *Romance*

Published by Silhouette Books New York

SILHOUETTE BOOKS, a Simon & Schuster Division of
GULF & WESTERN CORPORATION
1230 Avenue of the Americas, New York, N.Y 10020

Distributed by Pocket Books

ISBN: 0-671-57027-7

First Silhouette printing August, 1980

10 9 8 7 6 5 4 3 2 1

Printed in the U.S.A.

Chapter One

It was with a mixture of excitement and apprehension that Paula Blake looked down from the airplane to the coastline of the West Indian island of Puerto Rico. The excitement was due to the fact that she had never before been anywhere near the Caribbean, while the feeling of apprehension resulted from the fact that she had not yet met her employer, the Latin American gentleman whose name was Ramon Calzada Gonzalez, an eminent lawyer whose home was the Hacienda Calzada a few miles from the colonial town of Mayaquez, which was on the west coast of the island. The interview for the post of secretary had taken place at the Savoy Hotel in London, where Paula had been closely questioned by a Mrs. Glynn, a distant relation of the man whom Paula must address as Senor Calzada.

'We've had some excellent applicants,' said Mrs. Glynn, 'but you have been chosen, quite naturally, owing to your speaking Spanish.'

Paula had seen the advertisement in a London

newspaper and had answered it merely for interest, never for one moment expecting to get the post. And now, as she came nearer to her destination, her entire mind was occupied with her employer. Mrs. Glynn had said that she would be living in his house until she found her own accommodations, so naturally Paula was curious to know what he was like. A few ventured questions had brought forth the information that the man was very tall and dark. And he was handsome in a severe kind of way. Mrs. Glynn had added after a moment of considering, 'He's had several secretaries in the last two years but there were—er—problems and he decided to try an English girl.' Mrs. Glynn stopped and a small sigh escaped her. She looked speculatively at Paula and said bluntly, 'Don't make the mistake of falling in love with him, will you?'

Paula's chin went up.

'I have a boyfriend,' she returned shortly.

'Oh, well—that's good.' Another pause and then, 'He doesn't mind you leaving him? He is in England, I presume?'

'He's got a job on a cruise ship: it'll last two years, and then he's intending to settle down and manage his father's restaurant in Surrey.'

'I see. . . . And you, too, are wanting to see something of the world before you settle down?'

'Yes, that's the idea. I answered several advertisements before seeing this one. I had hoped to obtain a secretarial post in an hotel abroad.'

'Well, this post is better than any you'd have found in any hotel.'

Paula had hesitated before asking, 'Is Senor Calzada a bachelor?'

'Yes. At thirty-two he's still on his own.' The woman had paused then, a strange expression crossing her face which made Paula curious as to the woman's thoughts. She felt there was something concerning Mr Calzada which Mrs. Glynn was reluctant to reveal.

'These other secretaries . . . they fell in love with him?' It seemed an impertinence to ask a question like that but it had come unconsciously, and to Paula's relief Mrs. Glynn seemed not to consider it strange.

'I suppose I gave you that impression. It's true that they made nuisances of themselves, Miss Blake. Ramon was angry and rightly so. What man in his position wants an employee throwing herself at him all the time?'

Paula coloured. She resolved never to do or say anything that might be misconstrued. She was not interested in foreigners anyway—and especially Spaniards. They were too hot-blooded for her liking. She preferred simple, quiet men like Denis, with whom she had been keeping company for almost six months before he went off on the cruise ship. One day they might marry, but as yet marriage had never been mentioned. They had both wanted to do something interesting first, and were in perfect agreement about their respective plans.

Mrs. Glynn asked if she would be leaving Senor Calzada's employ when her young man returned to England for good.

'I'm not sure,' was Paula's frank reply.

'How did you come to learn Spanish?' queried Mrs. Glynn, changing the subject.

'I did it merely for a hobby—at night school.'

'It's served you in good stead.'

'Yes, indeed it has.'

Paula had asked again for information about her future employment, but had learned nothing more of the man himself, Mrs. Glynn having decided to describe the house in which Paula would be living. But first she had explained the Spanish custom regarding family names which was observed on the island.

'Ramon's father's name was Calzada,' she said. 'And his mother's Gonzalez, so he took both. You address him as Senor Calzada because it was his father's name.' Mrs. Glynn paused a moment then added, 'It was from his father that Ramon—Senor Calzada—inherited the vast estate, which is one of several in the district. The house dates back to the Spanish explorers but has undergone many important improvements since then. It's a noble mansion which captures the Golden Age of Spain in every single room,' continued the woman, carried away by enthusiasm. 'There are priceless tapestries on the walls, and paintings, of course. There is lovely antique furniture—I particularly love the ancient chests and poster beds. It's regal,' she went on, faintly amused by the awed expression that was creeping into her listener's eyes. 'Centuries slip by in seconds as you walk along the broad gallery of the inner court, or look out to graceful patios from beneath Renaissance arches. It's never difficult to imagine the proud and arrogant Spanish Grandees strutting along, viewing their exotic gardens—' She stopped a moment before adding, 'Ramon can almost be described as a throwback and you might find him exceedingly arrogant at times. I'm used to him, but to anyone who isn't, he can be rather overpowering. It depends on how he takes to you; he's an unpredictable man who finds fault easily. However,' she added with haste on noticing Paula's changed expression, 'I'm sure that you will get along fine with him.'

'I sincerely hope so,' had been Paula's heartfelt rejoinder. She had given up an excellent secretarial post, one that she could never hope to get again.

'I've given you all the instructions, haven't I?' asked Mrs. Glynn finally and Paula said yes, everything was clear to her. 'You do have to catch the other flight, since Ramon's place is some ninety miles or so from the International Airport of San Juan. You will fly to Mayagüez Airport where someone will meet you—probably José, Ramon's chauffeur.'

Paula's reverie was interrupted by the person sitting next to her saying, 'Do you mind if I lean over you and look down at the view?'

'No, of course not.'

'Tropical scenes fascinate me!'

'You've travelled widely?'

'A fair amount, but never to this island before.'

The woman sat down again and Paula brought out a compact from her handbag, surveying herself in the tiny mirror for a long moment as she thought again of her employer and found herself wondering if her appearance would satisfy him.

In the tiny mirror she saw a face of rare beauty set in a halo of tawny-gold hair, short and fringed and waving slightly. Her hazel eyes were large, framed by dark curling lashes which at times seemed to cast the kind of shadows that made them appear to be flecked with blue. Her mouth was wide and generous, her nose small, her chin pointed. At the age of twenty she had won a beauty competition; now, at twenty-four, there was about her features something stronger, a sort of classical quality that lent maturity to that earlier attractiveness. Denis had called her pretty, and had been chided by another young admirer of Paula's who was standing close by.

'Don't you know the difference between prettiness and beauty, Denis?' he had said, and Paula had coloured up and walked away without waiting to hear her boy-friend's response.

It was early evening when Paula arrived at Mayagüez Airport where she was met by the chauffeur, José, a swarthy-skinned man of Spanish-Indian descent. He was middle-aged and pleasant, speaking to her in Spanish as he asked if she had had a good journey. She answered him in Spanish and he beamed.

'You speak very good Spanish,' he said, in English.

The journey was not long; soon the huge car was entering through high wrought-iron gates with huge stone supports on each side and a coat-of-arms blazoned on top of them. Everything spoke of grandeur, of opulence, almost. It came as a shock to remember that Senor Calzada was a lawyer, working for his living.

She was taken by a maid in starched clothes to a saloon where she looked with admiration on some of the tapestries mentioned by her interviewer in London. The hacienda was high, being built on a knoll, and its views were breathtaking, with the sea not far away, its waters molten in the fiery rays of a lowering sun. Lush hills rose on the other side, darkened by shadows here and there where giant banyan trees formed barriers against the sunlight. There were tropical trees in the gardens, with orange groves in the distance. A few farm buildings could also be discerned, and farm workers' houses surrounding a rustic plaza. A small school shone pink in the sun's filtering light but Paula guessed that the walls were gleaming white in the light of dawn. Children were playing; they appeared like dolls in the distance and the swiftly-fading light. All was magic, unreal to a girl who had never seen anything remotely like it before.

Paula sighed contentedly, then turned from the window to confront her employer, Senor Calzada, who had entered silently. She stared, gasping inwardly. Mrs. Glynn had described him as handsome; she had never prepared Paula for this man who now stood in the room!

She continued to stare, not realising that he was staring too. She noticed the stern angular features, foreign, saturnine. The mouth was full, sensuous, the chin thrust forward, the eyes almost black, and piercingly intent. Paula's awed gaze took in the immaculately-clad figure—he wore a white linen suit and lilac shirt, frilled down the front, which carried not one ounce of surplus weight. And tall . . . ! He must be six-foot-three or four—Paula had never seen anyone quite so tall.

Suddenly she realised that he was staring as intently at her as she was at him, and a deep flush rose to her cheeks, making her angry because she was remembering that she had resolved not to do or say anything that could be misconstrued by her employer.

'*Buenas tardes, senorita.*' The voice was clipped and foreign-sounding. Paula managed to pull herself together and return his greeting, but she spoke in English.

'Good evening, senor.'

He came forward from the open doorway and extended a hand to her. There seemed to be fire in the depths of those dark eyes as he said, speaking flawless, accentless English which stamped him instantly as a complete bilingual,

'You had a good journey?'

'Very good, thank you, senor.'

'You must be tired, though. Your rooms are prepared; I'll have Magdalena show you up-stairs. Dinner is served at eight o'clock. I shall expect you to join me and then we can talk together.' The dark eyes still seemed to be on fire as they roved over her body from the delicate curve of her throat to her breasts and then to her waist and slender thighs. Her colour increased, for she felt like some desirable piece of merchandise which was being examined for possible flaws before purchase. The humour of that brought an involuntary smile to her lips and she saw him lift his brows in a gesture that could only be described as arrogance. The eyes glinted and the full mouth went tight. 'You're amused, senorita?' he said tautly, and she immediately shook her head.

'It was nothing,' she said.

'I abhor people who snigger for nothing, especially women!'

Her eyes opened wide at this outspokenness,

this utter rudeness which was totally unnecessary. But she could not retaliate, she dared not. The man overawed her, made her feel inferior, a mere nothing in his august presence. She glanced around and in imagination saw what Mrs. Glynn had described: the proud and arrogant Spanish Grandees strutting about, lords of all they surveyed, masters of the slaves over whom they ruled supreme.

'I was not sniggering, senor,' was all she said, but with a chill in her tone. Already she was concerned about the success of the venture. She was not used to being treated in this way, her previous employer being one of those men who considered his staff to be his equals.

Senor Calzada made no comment, but went over to an ornate bell-rope and pulled it. A dark-skinned girl came almost at once.

'Magdalena, show Senorita Blake to her suite.' The curtness of his voice was matched by the quality of indifference in his eyes as he turned them upon his new secretary. 'Make sure you are not late for dinner,' he added, and the next moment he was striding to the door.

'If you will come with me, senorita . . . ?' The girl was leading the way, having spoken in very broken English. Paula spoke to her in Spanish and she brightened. Obviously she had not expected the new guest to be able to speak her language.

The first room into which Paula was shown caused her to gasp. It was splendid to say the least, and surprisingly subdued both in its decor and its furnishings. On the walls were some paintings, mainly by contemporary artists, and on a side table of highly polished oak stood a beautiful Chelsea-Derby group. In the bedroom she found the same good taste and atmosphere of sheer wealth and luxury. The bathroom carried the same reflection, with its sunken bath surrounded by thick-pile carpet in a delicate shade of rose; the curtains matched and so did the towels. The lighting was concealed, one rose-coloured lamp being hidden within the foliage of a potted fern.

'You like these rooms, senorita?' Magdalena smiled expectantly. Paula nodded. They returned to the sitting-room and she went to the window, gazing out at the view. It was stupendous! The dark sea to one side and the hills to the other, in between were the gardens, immaculately kept, and where statuary gleamed in the saffron glow of the setting sun. Already lights were appearing in some of the tall trees, especially the lovely feathery sierra palms; and several fountains were stealing delightful colours from the dying rays of the sun. Paula turned, taking in the girl's appearance in one swift glance. Magdalena's figure was slender, almost immature. Paula guessed her age to be around eighteen.

'Yes, indeed,' she answered when the girl again asked if she liked the rooms. 'I'm very happy with my apartment.'

'Shall I unpack for you?' she asked as Paula went over to the door leading to the bedroom. 'José has brought up your suitcases, as you can see.'

'Yes, I'd like you to unpack for me,' answered Paula, glancing at the massive wardrobe on one high, satin-lined wall. 'I'll be having a bath.'

'Oh, then I will run the water for you first.'

Paula was puzzled. Surely she was not to be provided with a personal maid.

'What are your normal duties?' she inquired, turning at the bathroom door.

'I am new here, senorita, and my duties have not yet been told to me by the senor's housekeeper. I think I am a general helper with many things to do in the house.'

'I see.' Paula took her bath, her feelings mixed. She was troubled, now that she had met the man who was to be her employer. But within minutes she was to be more troubled than ever.

Magdalena seemed to be eager to open up a conversation and Paula, not wishing to snub the girl, and at the same time remembering that she herself was just as much an employee here as Magdalena, smiled with faint encouragement, expecting the girl to tell her about the island, or the people, or perhaps the recreations which Paula knew were by no means wanting in Puerto Rico. There was just about everything, she had been told. Magdalena mentioned none of these things. She said with interest, watching Paula's expression closely,

'What do you think of Senor Calzada? He is handsome, yes?' The girl spoke in Spanish, her whole manner expectant.

'Very.' Paula was alert, ready to put an end to the conversation if the girl became too familiar in her remarks about her employer.

'He has many affairs, but hates women, because of what his mother, sister and fiancée did to him. It is known that he hates women and yet they fall in love with him. Every one believes she will—what do you say, break down his—'

'Magdalena,' interrupted Paula gently, 'I don't

think you ought to be talking like this about
Senor Calzada.'

'Oh, but everybody talks about him,' returned
the maid, undaunted. She had a suitcase on a
chair and was taking out some blouses and
putting them on hangers. 'He is embittered and
vengeful with women—you understand? And he
is a rake now, but once he was a nice man.'

'You obviously heard all this as soon as you
came here?'

'No. Senor Calzada is talked about everywhere.'

That must surely be an exaggeration, decided
Paula, but she was frowning all the same. She
had expected to be working for a highly-
respected lawyer, and the noble owner of an
estate. Well, he was certainly the owner of an
estate, a vast one, but as for being highly-
respected, that was obviously not the case. She
said after a pause, 'I'm sure you are wrong when
you say he's talked about everywhere.'

The girl gave a small shrug. 'Most people
know about the affairs of Senor Calzada. He
lives in San Juan most of the time and it is there
that he has many lady friends.'

'San Juan?' Mrs. Glynn had not mentioned
anything about his living in the capital . . . and
yet she, Paula, ought to have surmised that he
would be practising in the main city of the
island, since most of the business would be
conducted there.

He was waiting when she entered the saloon to
which she had been conducted by Magdalena.
Paula stood for a moment just inside the door,
looking at him. It was easy to imagine his

having numerous affairs, because he possessed just about everything a man could possess. *He would stand out in any crowd, even among royalty,* she thought, advancing now into the room as his eyes widened in pompous, urbane enquiry as if he were asking why she was standing there, staring at him. He was still dressed in the same white linen suit with the frilled shirt. His black hair, waving away from his forehead, shone, and the same healthy sheen was on his dark skin. She saw his eyes wander, found herself anxious that she was looking her very best. Her dress was new, an evening gown of crisp cotton, white with vivid red flowers and bright green leaves, a slashed neckline and short cap sleeves. His eyes became fixed on the tightness of the bodice where it contoured her breasts in seductive beauty; she coloured, because she could not help it, and something stirred within her. She glanced down at his slender brown hands . . . and wondered why.

'You are early,' was his prosaic remark, which seemed to break the spell in which she was being caught. A long breath was let out; she found herself deliberately thinking of Denis, as if he were a safety valve of which she must never lose sight.

'I am usually punctual,' she returned, trying to smile but failing to do so.

'Can I get you a drink?' Already he was striding over to a cabinet, every step portraying pride and arrogance. The strain was already beginning to tell and Paula wished with all her heart that she had not accepted the post without first meeting her prospective employer. It had been a stupid thing to do, but at the time she was so thrilled to be going to the West Indies that she lost sight of the more important side of the contract.

'Yes, please,' she returned quietly. 'I'll have a dry Martini.'

He poured it for her, standing over her as he handed her the glass . . . standing far too close for her comfort.

'We shall talk over dinner.' His voice was clipped and aloof, and authoritative. 'There is much to discuss.'

'Yes, of course.' She accepted the glass, then took possession of the chair he indicated. What a magnificent specimen he was! She could not take her eyes off him, and was furious with herself at being affected so strongly by his appearance. But there was something magnetic about his personality as well, and again she brought out the mental picture of Denis, just to get herself back to reality. For Denis was real, an ordinary young man, whereas this nobleman standing here was more like a god, unapproachable. 'Mrs. Glynn did tell me a good deal about the post but, as I told her, I've never worked for a lawyer before.'

'I have her report,' he said. 'She was in constant touch by telephone while the proceedings were going on.'

'I see. So you know all there is to know about me.'

At that the first faint glimmer of a smile broke the hard and haughty outline of his mouth.

'I know nothing about you,' he murmured, the brilliant eyes narrowing slightly. He was standing in the middle of the room, his glass half-raised to his lips. 'You will talk to me about yourself over dinner.'

She frowned up at him and said tautly, 'You mean about my work, senor.'

'I mean about *you*, senorita.' The glass reached his mouth and he sipped the sherry contained in it. 'You're a very beautiful woman, Miss Blake,' he added in English. 'Are you engaged—or keeping company perhaps?' His eyes strayed to her left hand. He spoke again before she had time to answer. 'No, you have no fiancé, since it is not conceivable that he would allow you to come here and work for another man.' The tone had changed, taking on an edge that was unmistakably harsh, and Paula knew for sure that he was remembering his own fiancée. *What had she done to him*? Paula wondered. 'You are blushing, senorita,' he observed, again affording her no time to speak. 'It is because I said you are beautiful. But surely other men have said the same to you?'

She glanced away, angry and confused that he would speak to her this way. She said abruptly, 'I have a young man friend, senor. He and I decided we wanted to see something of the world before settling down, so he went on a cruise ship as steward and I took this post.'

'It is only temporary?' he queried sharply, his dark brow knitting in a sudden frown.

'I shall be with you for at least two years—' She broke off, aware that she was not answering with the truth. For she was unsure of herself, of her staying power with a man who was so vastly different from what she had expected. True, Mrs. Glynn had warned her of his probable arrogance, but this man was a rake too, and hard. She had admitted that he was handsome—the most superlatively attractive man she had ever met—but she also saw in his aristocratic features a certain harshness, cruelty, even. She had no doubts that Ramon Calzada Gonzalez had something as cold and inflexible as granite where his heart should have been. Never could she imagine his knowing what pity and compassion meant. Nor could she see him gentle and loving. She thought of all those women Magdalena had spoken of, and came to the instant conclusion that he would take them heartlessly and without a trace of emotion. Playthings, and despised; thrown aside to make way for more of their kind. Paula felt sickened all at once and would have done anything to be somewhere else. She decided that, over dinner, she would let him see that she was in doubt about working for him. Yes, she had taken on the job and she would stay until he got someone else—

'You were saying, senorita?' His voice, commanding, cut her thoughts; she glanced up into his dark forbidding face. 'You are intending to stay at least two years?'

'I—I . . .' Her lips were dry and she licked them unconsciously. 'I ought to have come over and met with you before I made up my mind.'

The dark eyes widened, regarded Paula disconcertingly, then narrowed again.

'You've had a change of heart?' He seemed unable to comprehend such an eventuality and Paula found difficulty in suppressing a smile. This was obviously a blow to his ego!

'I rather think the job will be unsuitable to me.' She frowned inwardly, thinking of all she had given up to take this post. Her job was gone; her flat was let on a one-year lease with the option to the tenant of a further year. What an upheaval there would be if she decided to go home.

'You haven't tried the work,' was his brusque rejoinder. 'How can you say it will not suit you?'

She looked at him curiously.

'Will *I* suit *you*?' she said. 'I know that you relied on Mrs. Glynn to find someone who would meet with your approval, but you must have known, senor, that there was a risk.'

'You are thinking that I ought to have gone over to England myself, and conducted the interviews?'

She nodded her head; she saw his eyes become focused upon her and was aware that the movement had caused her hair to catch the glow from a wall light just above the chair on which she was sitting.

'I feel it would have been better for us both.'

'You'd not have accepted the post had you met me before?'

She coloured and glanced away. She had tried to be tactful, but evidently he was not intending to do the same.

'I can't say for sure, senor,' she managed at last.

'Prevaricating? I am sure, Miss Blake,' he went on, reverting to English, 'that you would have refused to come and work for me.' A pause before he added, softly as if to himself, 'But, then, I rather think that I would never have offered you the post.'

Her eyes flew to his.

'You wouldn't?' she said.

'I have found that a beautiful girl is a pest,' he

returned bluntly. 'Too many men run after her. I hope, Miss Blake, that you will let it be known that you are spoken for.'

They dined in a high-ceilinged room of elegant but moderate proportions, dined by the light of twenty or more candles, all set in Waterford crystal holders; the chandeliers—of which there were three—were also of Waterford. The silver cutlery on the table was Georgian, from England; the porcelain was Wedgewood.

'You have all these from England?' Paula had to remark as she sat down.

'In San Juan one can buy products from all over the world, including antiques,' he told her, picking up a carved wooden basket containing warm crispy bread rolls. 'Try one; my chef is an expert on breads—as on everything else.' *He spoke matter-of-factly, as if he had been used to perfection, so long that he took it for granted and to be his right,* she thought, accepting a roll and putting it on to her side-plate. She touched the petal of an orchid that was contained, with others, in a Regency cut-glass salt-cellar which had been used as a miniature flower vase and which was set beside her wine glass.

'I had no idea that Puerto Rico was so modern,' she said.

'You thought—like many misinformed people—that we are living in near poverty?'

'I did believe that there was a great deal of poverty,' she admitted.

'You will very soon realise just how wrong you were.'

'I might not stay,' she was forced to remind him, to which she received a dark frown as he

said, 'You've signed a contract. I can keep you to
it.' Implacable the tone; she felt, though, that he
could do very little if she were to break that
contract.

'I know, but I feel that you'd not want me to
stay if I weren't happy.'

'Happy,' with a slight lift of one straight black
eyebrow. 'I am not concerned with the happiness of my employees,' he added with unveiled
indifference, as he took up his knife and began
to butter his roll. 'It is sufficient that I pay more
than is normal for any services rendered to me,
and there my interest comes to an end.' His long
slender fingers held the knife; Paula stared at
them, fascinated for some reason she could not
explain. She knew their slenderness and apparent delicacy was undoubtedly deceiving. 'I shall
expect you to honour the contract you have
signed,' he continued when she did not speak.
'You must at least give the work a trial.' There
was something in his voice that dominated in
the most subtle way. Paula knew she would
have to submit to his will, to honour the contract
she had so eagerly and unthinkingly signed.

Chapter Two

She was sitting in a shady arbour in the hacienda grounds, reading a letter received this morning from her mother, and redirected by the lessees of Paula's flat. It was over three months since Paula had written to her, telling her that she was contemplating taking a post somewhere abroad. The post of secretary to Senor Calzada had not come up at that time, and as yet Paula had not written to inform her mother of her change of work and residence; she had been awaiting an answer to her previous letter—and growing a little angry at the same time. For her mother was not one for writing, and to Paula that seemed selfish and unfair. She had been deprived of both father and mother when she was only eighteen because they had agreed to a divorce, each having met someone else. To Paula, who was a romantic and full of lovely ideals regarding the permanency of love and marriage, this had been little less than horrific. Bewilderment, unhappiness, insecurity . . . all had come with the suddenness of a summer storm and she had been torn apart, floundering, especially when her mother had said the home would be sold and she would find a nice little flat for her daughter. Within a couple of weeks of the divorce being made final, the second marriages were taking place. Paula was invited to both; she went to neither. Tears and more tears had been shed in the flat where she lived alone, her world crashed about her ears. But she possessed a certain strength and resilience which was bound to come to her aid in the end, and as she had a good post with the firm where she later worked as secretary to the managing director, she was eventually able to make some sort of a life for herself. She mixed with a crowd of young people and the mother of one insisted she enter the beauty contest which she had won. Confidence was the greatest profit, not the prize, but the prize came in handy too, as it bought some rather attractive pictures and ornaments for the flat. By the time she was twenty-one, Paula was happy in her independence, but she had never really forgiven her parents for the suddenness with which they had sprung their intentions upon her. She'd had no idea that they were interested in others, but she later extracted the information from her father that he had had another woman for over three years while his wife had been going out with someone else for about six months. Undoubtedly it was her father's conduct that had been responsible for her mother deciding to find someone else. Paula had never been considered by either of them.

And now, it was too much trouble for her mother to write regularly. Her father had written every month, but he had died just over a year ago, leaving everything to his wife. Although Paula had not wanted either his property or his money, she was bitter about being left out of the will. She ought to fight it, her friend's mother had advised wrathfully, but Paula had said no. Her father's wishes must be observed.

The letter was short, containing the news that her mother and stepfather were going to live in New Zealand.

'Perhaps, dear, you will visit us sometime,' was the vague invitation which disgusted Paula. 'I'll let you know our address as soon as I can, but we'll be busy, Paula, so don't be upset if there is some delay. However, we must keep in touch, mustn't we, dear?'

Keep in touch. . . . What a thing for a mother to say to her daughter! Crumbling the single sheet of paper into a ball, she tossed it away. She must retrieve it later, she mused, not because she wanted it, but because she ought not to have thrown it there, among the African violets.

She dozed, and on waking up forgot all about the letter. She went towards the house, her thoughts on her employer, who had been working steadily on a case for the whole of the fortnight she had been with him. He was defending a motorist accused of killing a cyclist by dangerous driving, the district court judge who held the hearing having decided that cause existed for criminal prosecution. For Paula the work had been extremely interesting, something entirely new, but it had been difficult as well, as Ramon Calzada had proved to be a hard taskmaster, just as she had expected. But she felt certain that he was satisfied with her, and she was determined that he should continue to be satisfied.

Her thoughts switched from his work to his pleasure.

One evening a woman had arrived, driving a large car; she was about thirty years of age and possessed a dark, exotic beauty which, thought Paula, *would appeal to any man*. She was obviously of Latin American origin, but her eyes gave evidence of a hint of the Orient somewhere along the genetic line. Ramon had smiled thinly as he introduced the girl to Paula, and Paula decided that the woman had no pride to be treated with what amounted almost to indifference. Paula was not invited to dine with them, but she had not expected to be, since she had dined with her employer only twice—once on the first evening, and the second time a couple of nights later when he said he wanted to give her a full outline of what he was doing so that when she was typing the details of the case she would have a better understanding of it.

The woman, whose visit seemed to depress Paula in some indefinable way, had stayed the night, ostensibly occupying the guest suite, but Magdalena was quick to tell Paula that the bed, although ruffled, had not been slept in.

'The senor has a big double bed in his room,' she had added, before Paula, trying not to appear embarrassed, told the girl that she was not interested in the private affairs of the senor.

'Senorita Cuevas is his latest—what do you say? Flirt?'

'I've already said I am not interested, Magdalena!'

'Sorry, senorita! I won't do it again.'

Not until the next time, thought Paula grimly, wondering how she was going to stop the girl's tongue.

Paula had thought about Maria Cuevas a great deal since that night, finding it strange that she should come to Ramon, rather than that he should go to her. Was she so crazy about him that she must run after him? Surely her action amounted to nothing less than that. No wonder he had an inflated opinion of himself! What he wanted was a set-down—for some young lady to scorn his advances, to tell him that he was just not her type. Paula had to smile, for surely no woman breathing could say with honesty that Ramon Calzada did not attract her. As for Paula herself—she had to admit to his attraction, and she did have the greatest difficulty in ignoring it. Denis still served as her safety valve, and just so that she would not forget it she had brought a small frame for a snapshot she had once taken of him, and she now had this on her dressing-table.

Her thoughts reverted to the letter she had received and she turned, retracing her steps with the intention of picking it up from the bed of violets into which she had tossed it. It was not there, and she surmised it had been blown away by the breeze. But when she got back to the house the letter—having been straightened out—was handed to her by her employer. He was sitting on a marble terrace with the open window of the sitting-room behind him, and he looked totally relaxed. It was Saturday and he did not work on weekends unless it was vital.

'There's a letter of yours here, senorita.' He had called to her as she was passing, and in his hand was the letter. She came up the steps and took it, wondering if he had read any of it. 'Jorge found it and felt it might be important.'

'Thank you.' Jorge was the head gardener, and as he spoke no English he could not possibly have read it. Not that it would have mattered if he had, since there was nothing in it which was either important or confidential.

'You did not tell me that you had a stepfather,' said Ramon, eyeing her curiously.

'There was no need—' She stopped, then added, 'You have read my letter?'

'Jorge had straightened it out and the beginning caught my eye,' he answered casually. 'The end also caught my eye,' he added, and again his gaze was one of curiosity. 'Sit down,' he invited unexpectedly, then stood up and brought forward a lounger for her. She sat down; it was the first time they had sat together like this and it seemed far too intimate for an employer and his secretary. The letter was folded now and she slipped it into her pocket. 'When I asked you to tell me about yourself, that first evening, you left a lot out, I'm thinking.'

'Of course. I merely told you about my work and my life at home.'

'You said your parents were divorced, but you did not say that your mother had married again.'

'There was no need,' she repeated, puzzled by his interest in her affairs.

'Your mother asks you to keep in touch. Not much affection there—' He stopped so abruptly that Paula was startled. His eyes glittered and

his sensuous mouth was now a thin, cruel line.
Paula, watching his expression become harsh,
recalled what Magdalena had said about his
hating women because of what his mother had
done. 'You're not embittered,' he stated at last,
and there was an edge of contempt to his voice
as if he could find nothing praiseworthy in her
attitude.

'I was bitter at first,' she owned, apparently
surprising him. 'But now—well, I don't care.
I've made my own life and it doesn't really
matter about the past, does it?' Her voice was
serious and quiet, her gaze wide and honest,
concealing nothing. He stared at her with an
unfathomable expression in his brilliant dark
eyes, stared so hard and searchingly that she felt
the colour rise to tint her cheeks. The moment
was tense, electric, and Paula felt the flutterings
of a new sensation, the quickening of a pulse.
The palms of her hands became damp for no
reason at all and she found herself taking out a
handkerchief and pressing it between them. Her
employer's glance flickered to them for a second
before returning to her face.

'The past doesn't matter, you say?' He spoke in
English, cultured English which Paula had
found attractive right from the start.

'Not to me,' she answered. 'After all, each and
every one of us has a life to live which is our
very own, and to brood on what others have
done is not only profitless but unfair to them.'

He frowned in silence for a long moment
before saying, 'Unfair? When someone has
wronged you?'

'My parents had their own lives to live.'

'Parents have an obligation to their children.'

'That's true, and as I have said, I was bitter at first. But one can't go on being bitter.'

The dark face took on a brooding expression that was a revelation in itself. This man *was* unhappy! And the reason was that he had remained bitter, hating all women because of something his mother had done to him—and not only her, but his sister and his fiancée.

She regarded him closely, her curiosity such that had Magdalena offered information at this moment she would have been quite unable to resist listening to her—presupposing they were alone, that was.

'Am I to understand that you have forgiven your parents?' said Ramon at last, and Paula told him that her father was dead.

'As for my mother—I feel indifferent about her—' She stopped and a certain quality of sadness brought shadows to her eyes. 'I would have liked to have my mother's love,' she added finally, totally unaware of the catch in her voice, or the regret born of a deep, deep yearning to be wanted and needed. There was no one in the whole world who really needed her and the thought stabbed pain into her heart.

Ramon said after a long while, 'This young man you spoke about—will you marry him one day?'

'I'm not sure,' she replied candidly. 'He hasn't asked me for one thing.' The ghost of a smile accompanied this piece of information. 'He might meet someone else on his travels.'

'You wouldn't mind?'

'He has his own life to live,' she said, and now

she felt sure he was thinking of his fiancée, the girl who had obviously let him down some time in the past.

'You appear to be very philosophical about life, and people.'

'And about what they do to me?' Half-statement, but half-question as well. This conversation bordered on the intimate, but the whole situation was intimate, different from any that had gone before when he was her cool dispassionate employer and she his secretary, reserved and a little fearful of not doing the right thing.

'Yes,' he said, 'about what they do to you. I'm afraid I can't be so dispassionate about it.'

She hesitated, wondering if she dare say what was in her mind. She did say it, but with a hint of apology which she hoped would allay any anger he might otherwise have evinced.

'I think it is because you are what you are, senor.'

His brows shot up. 'Meaning that I am not derived from such stolid stock as you?'

She had to laugh. 'Something like that,' she admitted. 'The Spanish are not so cool and calm as the English— But I would not describe my people as stolid,' she added defensively.

'There is no fire in them,' he returned, a challenge in his expression.

She gave a small shrug.

'What is fire, senor?' she asked unthinkingly.

It was his turn to smile, such an attractive smile that Paula instinctively caught her breath.

'Are you asking me to show you, senorita?'

The blood rushed to her cheeks.

'I—I don't know what you—you mean. . . .'

The dark eyes stared into hers for a space before his lashes came down; Paula, filled suddenly with a sense of humiliation, knew instinctively that, had those thick lashes not effectively hidden his expression, she would have read contempt within it, and this time it had nothing to do with the way she felt about her mother. No, it was because he believed she had tried to flirt with him, saying as she had, 'What is fire, senor?'

With a lift of her chin she told him he had misunderstood her.

'I was merely being conversational,' she almost snapped and rose from the chair. Anger seethed within her; she had been enjoying the conversation, content to be here on the sunny terrace with the flower perfumes from the garden invading the air around her, assailing her nostrils, as the hum of busy insects assailed her ears. 'I'll go. And thank you for my letter!'

She had already turned away when his voice said authoritatively, 'Sit down.'

She stopped in her tracks.

'I have things to do,' she said over her shoulder.

'Sit down. . . .' The voice soft, commanding and suddenly very foreign to her ears. 'Senorita,' he added when she did not instantly do his bidding, 'I am used to implicit obedience from those whom I employ. Sit down.'

She swung around, swallowing convulsively and running her tongue over her lips that had suddenly gone dry. He was staring at her from his comfortable place on the lounger, his eyes narrowed and arrogantly flicking over her figure.

'Senor,' she began huskily, 'I understood that the weekends were my own. It's Saturday and—'

'Senorita, you are asking for dismissal!' No longer was the voice soft; it was harsh and imperious. 'Obey me—at once!'

She sat down, fury in her veins. Dismissal! She had a good mind to give him her notice!'

'I don't understand what this is all about,' she managed when he did not speak. 'I am not obliged to sit here, with you, on my days off.'

'But you are obliged to treat me with respect! Your action in bringing our conversation to such an abrupt termination was insolent! I expect an apology from you.'

She stared, his words repeating themselves in her mind. They were so stiff and formal and she wondered if the man was ever able to unbend. She had been with him for two weeks and never for one single moment had she seen him betray an atom of emotion. And now . . . he was sitting there, relaxed it was true, but like a statue made of stone. She shook her head, reluctant to make the apology he was demanding. But, somehow, she found herself weakening beneath that haughty and imperious stare. A sensation of inferiority took the place of her anger and she heard herself say, in a low tone that was almost meek, 'I'm sorry, senor. I meant no offence.'

'You will remember in future that I demand respect—all the time, whether you are on duty or not.'

'Yes, senor.' He said nothing and she murmured presently, 'I haven't yet tried to find accommodations. Do I advertise, or—?'

'You will remain here for the time being,' he broke in authoritatively. 'We shall be leaving for San Juan on Tuesday. I have an office there. I also have a house.'

'A house? You mean—' She shook her head vigorously. 'I can't stay there!'

'It's a very large house,' he explained reassuringly. 'And I have a housekeeper in residence.'

'Oh . . .' She still disliked the idea of living under his roof, but made no further objection, at least not about accommodation in San Juan. Here, however, she preferred to have her own house or flat. She told him so but he shook his head.

'We shall be constantly moving back and forth, it's usual,' he said. 'It would be a waste for you to pay out money for a flat here.'

'Mrs. Glynn made me understand that I was here, in your house, only temporarily, until I found a place of my own.'

'I prefer to have you under my roof,' he returned inexorably. 'There will be occasions when I shall want you to work in the evenings, or even on weekends. You will, of course, have time off to compensate.'

She drew a breath, feeling trapped in the net of this man's domination. Never had she expected to be treated like this—domineered and dictated to as if she had no will of her own. There had been no mention, at the interview, of her having to work on the weekends and perhaps some evenings, but on reflection Paula rather thought that her employer had not considered it necessary for Mrs. Glynn to be in possession of every detail. The successful applicant would learn all about the post once she arrived here.

Should she leave? The salary was exceptionally good, and in addition she had free accommodation and food. In fact, everything she earned was profit, and she would be able to save practically the whole of it. And should Denis want to marry her, she would be able to make a substantial contribution to the expenses of setting up a home. Yes, there were many advantages to this post, and after all, nothing in life was perfect. She had once read that there was no such thing as a happy life, but merely happy moments, and for a long time now Paula had accepted this as the truth.

Ramon's house in *Viejo San Juan*—the Old San Juan—was a revelation to Paula, something she had never expected. But every single thing about this ancient and historic city was fascinating: its fortress built by the Spanish over a period of two-hundred-and-forty-four years to ensure impregnability against attacks from determined European rivals; its blue cobblestones, brought to the island as ballast in the galleons of ancient Spain; its narrow streets faced with centuries-old buildings whose handsome iron and wooden balconies were hung with myriads of exotic, flowering plants. The powerful fortress of San Cristobal seemed to dominate the whole city, with Fort El Morro at the far point, its massive walls at one time being the shelter for the treasure galleons of Imperial Spain.

The Casa Don Felipe—Ramon's house on Cristo Street—was an eighteenth-century Spanish colonial townhouse, beautifully restored by a previous owner. It had balconies across the façade, a wide entrance hall hung with tapestries and armour, from which rose a wide, spectacular staircase. There were interior patios and high ceilings supported by hand-hewn beams made from the ausubo tree. A courtyard was paved with the coloured stone of Spanish times, and in the centre a fountain played, its sunlit spray settling into an ornamental pool with water lilies and other aquatic plants.

'It's . . . wonderful. . . .' breathed Paula gazing around. 'I never expected it to be like this.'

'In Old San Juan almost everything has been restored,' was all her employer said. He was not particularly gratified by her appreciation, since he had no interest in her reaction one way or another. He often seemed miles away, distant in thought—except for that one occasion when he had made Paula sit with him on the terrace and the conversation had become rather intimate. She had the impression of bitterness always, and thought many times of what she had been told by the maid, Magdalena.

This lovely house ought to be in the possession of someone different, she thought. For here was mellow warmth and the atmosphere of beauty preserved through many troubled times. Here was peace and tranquility found in shady nooks where the cool breeze brought the tang of the sea to mingle with exotic flower perfumes. All this belonging to a man who seemed unable to appreciate it, unable to gather from its bountiful resources something of its unique atmosphere. Not for Paula this disinterest! She adored it from the moment of entering the gates, just as, in a very short time, she was to come to adore the incredibly attractive city of Old San Juan, the second oldest city in the western hemisphere.

But exploring the city was not for the immediate present; very soon she was working hard, going out with Ramon every morning to his luxurious office, which was in the more modern city of San Juan. The work was interesting, with two visits to court where the proceedings were conducted exclusively in Spanish. These two cases had nothing to do with the major case resulting from the accident, and it was on this that Ramon was working very hard. Paula guessed that he considered his client to be innocent of any crime, and just over a week after they had moved to the city he told Paula that they would be going to the El Yunque Rain Forest where the accident had occurred.

'I want to see the exact spot,' he told her, 'and to take some pictures and measurements. You'll come with me and take it all down, then type it up for my files.'

'The accident happened in a forest?' she said, puzzled.

'There are good roads through El Yunque, there have to be, since it covers a great area, around twenty-eight thousand acres of tropical forest.'

'It must be vast!'

'Of course it's vast. You'll need suitable clothing,' he added. 'It isn't called the Rain Forest for nothing.'

'When are we going?'

'Friday, the day after tomorrow.' They were in the Blue and Gold Saloon, as it was called by

Ramon's housekeeper, Adela, a buxom, middle-aged woman with straight black hair and dusky skin. She had come to him from a nearby English-speaking island and was bilingual like her employer. She was proud to be holding the position of housekeeper to such an eminent lawyer, and a nobleman at that.

'I will never be stolen from him,' she had told Paula who, naturally asking what that meant, learned that maid stealing was a rather popular way of getting the help which, like everywhere else, was becoming more difficult all the time. She was busy with the dinner and Ramon and Paula were drinking cocktails as they waited for the little maid, Ana, to come to tell them that the meal was ready. Ana was a country girl whom Ramon had managed to get by sending his housekeeper into the country to search for someone whom she would find suitable. Ana's parents had approved and consequently released her into Adela's custody. She was shy but, said Ramon cynically, she would not be like that for long.

'Shall we be staying in the Rain Forest?' Paula asked, not quite knowing where it was or how long Ramon's investigations would take. 'There are hotels?'

'We won't be staying. It's only twenty-five miles from here, so we shall have plenty of time; in any case, if I don't do all I want to do on Friday, we can go back again on Monday.'

The telephone rang and he went over to it. Paula watched him, taking in the perfection of his face and figure, and the exquisite cut of his clothes. He always changed for dinner, and on those occasions when she dined with him she

was expected to do the same. Since coming here,
to San Juan, she had dined with him every
evening, and the result was that she and he
seemed to be getting to know one another far
more intimately than would have been the case
if she had had her own accommodation in some
other part of the city. She was finding difficulty
at times in ignoring his attraction, her mind
seeming to have no will of its own, as she tried to
steel herself against new emotions which had
begun to surface with palpable force, and which
seemed to be drawing her irresistibly to him,
despite the fact that she knew of his reputation
and deplored his way of life.

The picture of Denis was fading, so that it was
no longer easy to superimpose his image upon
that of Ramon. She had seen Ramon with an
American girl chatting in the office as if they
were old friends, and the stab that shot through
Paula's body was a sensation tantalisingly unex-
plained. She had been disturbed by it, and
although as yet she refused to allow it to come
totally to the forefront of her mind, she knew
with vague unease that, very soon, she was
going to be forced to analyse her feelings towards her employer.

He was speaking to some woman; she listened, still watching his face. But it was in
profile, the chiselled lines telling her nothing
and the lips did not smile even when he said, 'I
like your humour, Carmen. You have a most
diverting turn of phrase.'

Carmen. . . . So this was another, as Senorita
Cuevas's name was Maria.

Undoubtedly he was a no-good, a womaniser

of the most detestable kind, having several women at once like this.

'You have?' he was saying, still in that same unemotional tone. 'And it's just what you wanted?'

Silence while he listened, his eyes straying towards the chair where his secretary was sitting. She rose automatically and would have left the room but he waved an abrupt hand, indicating that she should sit down again.

'I must come over and see it. Tomorrow evening.' Curt the tone, and the last two words that should have been a question were a statement, a firm decision. So Carmen had been told he would visit her, not asked if it would be convenient.

The dinner was served in a high-ceilinged room with long windows draped in velvet and looking out on to the moonlit courtyard. Candles and flowers and gleaming glass on the table. Adela had trained her apprentice well, for it was Ana who had prepared the table and lit the candles. She had probably arranged the flowers, too. And if so, then she had a natural flair for the art, decided Paula as she sat down, having had her chair drawn out for her by Ramon. He had to come close, of course, as he pushed it back for her and she felt his cool breath on her cheek. Her pulse quickened and colour fused her face. His hand was close and those long lean fingers fascinated her.

She admitted, not without a sense of shock, that she would like to have experienced the feel of them, to know the contact of flesh with flesh. . . .

'You're blushing?' He stared questioningly as he took the chair opposite to her. 'Tell me why?'

Her eyes narrowed, for she was very sure that he knew why she was blushing.

'I didn't know I was,' she lied, her glance going deliberately to the window and the fountain bathed in light outside it. 'I don't often blush,' she added after a space.

'Women these days rarely do,' he agreed. 'But you—you're different. You've not been around, I think?'

'Around?' She knew very well what he meant but feigned ignorance.

He smiled a little mockingly. 'You've not had much experience of men.'

'No, I haven't, not in the way you mean.'

'And what way is that?'

She averted her head, hiding her expression. 'I believe you meant—er—affairs.'

To her surprise he laughed. She glanced up swiftly, her heart giving a little jerk. The laugh was in his eyes, and crinkly lines fanned out from the sides, adding to his attractiveness. Strong white teeth were still revealed as the laugh subsided to a smile.

'An innocent, eh? How refreshing! I'd never have believed that, at your age, you'd not tasted the sweet things of life.'

Her mouth set, because of her anger at his familiarity. 'Senor, can we change this topic to something else? Would you please tell me more about this journey we're making into the Rain Forest?'

'And shy as well. What is this young man of yours made of?'

'He knows what control is! And decency!'

'I've made you angry. I'm sorry.'

She looked at him in surprise, and he laughed again. No, he said, he did not often apologise to anyone. She must consider herself honoured.

After that the evening progressed pleasantly, with the conversation sometimes touching on the trip to El Yunque and sometimes on the other cases which Ramon had in hand.

At half-past ten Paula said she was going to bed. Ramon got up as she did, and for a moment they were staring at one another, Ramon's manner incomprehensible, his handsome face a mask as hard as stone.

'Good night,' she faltered, every nerve end quivering.

'Good night, senorita. Sleep well.' He opened the door for her but she did not move. Fear struck her unexpectedly; she was convinced that he would take hold of her as she went past him to leave the room. 'Something wrong?' he demanded, frowning in puzzlement.

'N-no. . . .' Rousing herself, she managed to cross the room. 'Th-thank you, senor,' she murmured, her whole body tensed as she came abreast of him. 'Good night,' she said again, looking up into his face.

He said nothing, and in seconds after she had passed him she heard the door close. Later, as she looked down from the wooden balcony of her bedroom, she heard music from below. He was listening to a recording of Beethoven's Symphony Number Five.

A strange man, unpredictable as Mrs. Glynn had said. An embittered man who seemed to be drifting through life without an aim . . . a man unloved . . . ?

Chapter Three

The following evening Ramon went out and he had not returned when Paula, denied sleep for some reason she could nót understand, turned out her bedlight at half-past one in the morning. She knew he had not returned because her ears had been alert for his passing her door, which he had to do to get to his own room farther along the corridor. Adela had cooked a delicious meal for Paula but she had no appetite and was obliged to apologise to the housekeeper who immediately asked if she were not feeling well.

'I'm all right, but not hungry,' she said. 'I think I'll go to bed.' And all she did was lie there, wondering what was the matter with her. She was disturbed in a way she could not fathom, and impatient with herself because of it. She was restless often in the office, when she was working with Ramon; she became more restless when those brilliant dark eyes rested on her, as they often did of late.

That he affected her as she had never been affected before she freely admitted, and she

did wonder if she ought to leave his employ and
return to England. Her mind was muddled,
owing to her previous decision to stay, and to
save furiously in case Denis should want to
marry her in two years' time.

But she was not now sure that she wanted to
marry him. . . .

The sun was streaming into the courtyard
when she got up and went to the window. It was
a restful sight that met her gaze, with the
fountain taking colour from the sun to create
rainbows which in turn caught the light. Fra-
grant white ginger grew in the shade of a
poinsettia tree, and in another part of the courtyard the shaded ground was dramatized by
delightful rose and pink flowers of the Impatient
Sultaness. Perfumes drifted up, assailing Paula's nostrils as she stepped out on to the balcony.
A sigh escaped her; all this beauty and she was
feeling unhappy.

'What on earth is the matter with me?' she was
saying as she lay in the scented bath water a few
minutes later. 'I was so thrilled when I got this
job.'

Ramon was not in the morning-room when
she entered for breakfast, and when she asked
Ana where he was the girl answered, in Spanish, 'He did not come home all night. I thought
perhaps he had an accident, but when I said this
to Adela she said no, it was quite all right. The
senor often did not come home. I think there was
a telephone message for you,' added Ana as if
suddenly remembering to mention the matter.

'Thank you, Ana. Has Adela got it?'

'Yes, I think so.'

Paula tried to eat but again she had no appetite for food. For some inexplicable reason she felt physically and mentally drained, as if an upheaval had taken place in her life. It was like this, she recalled, at the time her parents had sprung it on her that she was on her own, as they had both found other spouses and, inevitably, they must all part company.

Paula felt neglected and had fallen into a web of dejection at the idea of being entirely alone. But why should she feel the same way again? She was not alone altogether, there was still Denis who would surely be writing to her soon, as she had already sent her address to the ship on which he was working.

Adela gave her the message. She was to proceed to the office on her own, taking a taxi. 'I will call it for you,' offered Adela, but Paula said she would walk.

'I've plenty of time,' she added, managing a smile. 'I rather enjoy walking in the city.'

This morning there was no enjoyment, though, and when she arrived at the office to find that her employer had not arrived a girdle of dejection surrounded her.

It was time, she decided, to analyse her feelings for the man who was obviously a profligate, a man whom any sensible girl would avoid like the plague. . . .

He arrived soon after she did, looking cool and calm and faintly bored.

He bade her good morning, his hawk-sharp glance seeming to take in her depression because a slight frown creased his brow as he added, 'You're all right? Adela looked after you last evening?'

'Yes, of course she did.' Paula turned away, to

settle down at her desk and after a silent, unfathomable moment during which Paula was acutely conscious of his eyes on her bent head, he left the office to enter his own.

Paula sat beside her employer as he drove the car out of San Juan and along Route Three. He was silent, his handsome, Latin American features an expressionless mask. He seemed to be lost in thought, and Paula might as well not have been there, sitting beside him. She was not feeling particularly happy, mainly owing to the awareness of the powerful attraction she had for her employer. It was no use pretending, no use continuing to thrust off what was undoubtedly there: she was falling in love with Ramon Calzada . . . and now was the time to make her escape, before she was inflicted with irreparable hurt.

She had the greatest difficulty in understanding herself, for it was more than glaringly evident that even if he did by some miracle become interested in her it would be for one thing only: a swift and casual affair.

Determinedly she switched her thoughts, glancing through the side window of the car to take in the scenery. Ramon had turned on to Route One-ninety-one and they were climbing up El Yunque, into the Caribbean National Forest. Forgetting all else in the wonders of nature surrounding her, Paula stared and stared, catching her breath as the car ascended into the cool, magical atmosphere of one of the most beautiful and luxuriant rain forests of the world.

'It's wonderful,' she breathed, turning impulsively to her employer. 'I'd love to come up here and explore! There must be trails one can follow?'

'Of course.' He turned his head. She felt his swift appraising look before he applied his attention to the road again.

'You have nothing like this in your country?'

'No, we don't get this amount of rain.' As her companion made no further comment Paula fell silent, her mind almost drugged by the rare, inescapable impressiveness of the landscape. She had never even imagined anything so magically unreal, so cool and primitive. As a bend was taken, the scene before her brought another gasp to her lips. Falling from a great height, caught in the sunlight, millions of gallons of crystal-clear water cascaded down from the mountainside to spume and swirl, then drop again after flowing beneath the road.

'There are many waterfalls like that,' was Ramon's only response to the audible exclamation that issued from Paula's lips. Giant ferns reared up along the roadside; brilliant emerald vines entangled themselves inextricably among the branches of the trees that clothed the massif of El Yunque. The flashes of brilliant colour proclaimed the presence of parrots moving among the trees. 'Perhaps you would like to go to the observation tower?' suggested Ramon, surprising her.

'Yes, please! The view must be exceptional.'

'It is.'

On their arrival there he remained silent, but his whole attention was with Paula, his dark eyes probing into hers if she should happen to look his way.

Yet she almost forgot his presence as she

stood, her eyes wide with wonderment, looking down over the emerald landscape which swept in gentle undulations down to a fantastically beautiful beach fringed with palms.

'Come,' said her employer briskly at last, 'we have work to do.'

He knew the exact spot where the accident had occurred, and after parking the car on the side of the road he got out. For the next hour he was walking about, measuring the road, the angles, while Paula wrote down all he was saying. Watching him intently, she saw his mouth become tight; his eyes, unfathomable as ever, moved about, taking in everything— almost every feature of the road and the forest on either side of it.

She saw him nod his head and wondered what he had discovered.

'Are you satisfied with what you have found out?' she ventured to ask.

'Fairly. It is impossible to reconstruct an accident that took place up here, without a witness.'

'But you still believe your client to be innocent?'

'He is innocent,' was all Ramon said, and a few minutes later they were again in the car going back towards the restaurant where they had lunch of beef kebab roasted on a spit with a potato baked in its jacket. There were a few tourists, all Americans, all armed with mackintoshes. And they needed them. Ramon and Paula had barely covered two miles of the return journey when the rain came—a torrential tropical downpour which reduced visibility almost to nil and Ramon stopped the car.

'It's terrific!' Paula shook her head in disbelief. If the heavens had opened wide there could not have been more water emptied on to the forest. She thought of the lovely orchids she had seen and felt they must surely be destroyed by the sheer weight and force of the deluge pouring over them. She remarked on this to Ramon and received the terse reply that more orchids would grow to replace what were destroyed. His tone was casual; she felt sure he had no more feeling for flowers and other growing things than he had for the women who flitted through his life.

Suddenly he turned to her and surprised her by saying they would be dining out that evening. He was entertaining a client and his wife and Paula would be required to make a fourth at dinner.

The place chosen proved to be the most luxurious hotel in Old San Juan, a renovated convent, with the interior decor and furnishings savouring of a Spanish Renaissance castle. The lobby was a treasure chest of antiques and so was the lounge where there were ancient wooden chests, elaborately-carved occasional tables, tapestries on the walls and old, hand-woven rugs on the floors. Paula's dress, which she had managed to buy at a greatly reduced price in a sale, was of French manufacture. Fine printed cotton in white and duck-egg blue, it had a full pleated skirt and tight-fitting bodice held up with a halter. An antique silver bracelet and silver ring were her only pieces of jewellery. She had been to the rest room and used exotic perfume, and as she met her employer in the lounge she sensed the slight movement of his nostrils, as if he were taking in the perfume. She managed a quivering smile which brought forth no response. And not for the first time Paula was wondering if her employer ever dropped that cold, inflexible exterior and became human.

'We're rather early,' he said. 'Sit down. We'll have a drink while we're waiting.'

She took possession of a chair and leant back, watching his impassive countenance as he gave the order to the waiter. He seemed immune to the attractions of lights playing on the various exotic plants, on the fountain, or even to the Spanish accordion player attired in colourful dress.

The drinks arrived and then he did speak, to say that they would be returning to the hacienda on the following Thursday and would spend a long weekend there.

'Shall we be working for part of the time?' she asked, picking up her drink and absently moving her glass so that the ice tinkled against the side.

'Perhaps.' He looked keenly at her, his dark eyes having first flicked over her lovely figure. 'You have been working a good many extra hours lately; I might let you have the Friday off.'

'Thank you.' She paused, and then, 'Can I look for a place of my own?'

He shook his head at once.

'I have already said it isn't practical.'

'You can't want me in your home indefinitely,' she said.

'Your presence does not trouble me in the least.' With unveiled indifference he picked up his glass and sipped his aperitif.

'I would very much like to have my own place,' she persisted. Vitally aware of her weakness where his attractions were concerned, *it would be far better if she left altogether,* she thought, but if not that, then at least she must leave his home.

'I'd rather have you under my eye,' he said, and Paula frowned and opened her mouth. But she soon closed it again on noting his expression, which was forbidding to say the least. If that were not enough there was a stern inflection of finality in his next words. 'Local girls are not allowed the freedom of the women in your country. While you are here you will be subject to the same restrictions which I would put upon a sister.' His firmness was absolute. Paula decided there was no argument against it and subsided into silence. 'Is there any special reason for your aversion to living at the hacienda?' he added after a pause.

She felt the colour rise to her cheeks, and saw a fractional lift of his brows. The dark foreign eyes were impassive and yet she did wonder if, with his almost uncanny perception, he had guessed at her reason.

'It's just that a woman likes her own place,' she answered hastily. 'To live in another person's home is not the same.' She glanced at him from under her lashes, still afraid he might have guessed at her feelings . . . guessed that she was falling in love with him. No, he must not! It would be too humiliating. He would consider her to be no different from those others with whom he had become so impatient that he had decided to try an English woman, probably because, as he had declared, the English were cold.

'Her own place. . . .' The words came slowly, thoughtfully, while his foreign eyes remained focused on her face. He nodded slightly, as if something in his mind appealed to him. Paula, bewildered by his manner, picked up her glass and took rather more than she ought. 'Ah, here is my client and his wife.' Ramon made the introductions, and after a few seconds Paula found herself in conversation with Helena Perez, a glamorous brunette possessed of thoroughly patrician features and a spontaneity which Paula found both appealing and overwhelming at the same time, while Ramon was chatting with Don Luis, his client.

But the conversations were soon interrupted by the appearance of a waiter with the menu and for a short period of time the various dishes were discussed, mainly for Paula's benefit.

The Dining Terrace of the hotel overlooked the starlit harbour where the panorama of night-life had as its backdrop the hills highlighted by the glowing illuminations of the town. Along the waterfront many small cafés flaunted their signs, all advertising the best sea food on the island. There was movement and music and a magical blending of form and colour as the twinkling lights from the waterfront melded with the moonbeams glittering on the tranquil sea. All this complemented the romantic, candlelit ambiance of the Dining Terrace itself.

Paula chose flounder stuffed with crab as a starter, and this was followed by lamb cutlets with artichokes and water chestnuts. The other three preferred red wine and Ramon, remembering that Paula did not like red wine, ordered her a half bottle of dry white. She looked at him in surprise and saw a look of sardonic amusement in his eyes.

The evening passed pleasantly, but all the

time Paula was on tenterhooks without knowing why. Every glance sent by her employer unnerved her, gave her a skin-prickling feeling as of something unexpected pending.

But as she and Ramon drove back into the town her uneasiness fell from her because, as always, she was savouring the beguiling atmosphere of mellowness and age which the city exuded. But there was evidence too, of the cosmopolitan culture which seemed totally at variance with the unspoiled beauty of the island in general.

The housekeeper had gone to bed when they arrived back at the Casa Don Felipe and so had Ana. Paula thanked her employer for the wonderful dinner and turned to go.

'You enjoyed it?' Although his words revealed interest, there was an abstracted expression on his lean aquiline features.

'Yes, very much.'

'You looked most charming and sophisticated,' he commented, surprising her.

'Thank you,' she murmured, all her awkwardness returning. 'I—think it's time I was going to bed.'

'Come out onto the balcony with me.' His brusque tones overrode any protest she might have considered making and she acquiesced, nerves tingling. One half of her wanted to escape . . . but the other half wanted to go out there, into that romantic, moonlit setting, and be alone with her handsome employer.

'It's a beautiful night,' she murmured, more for something to say than anything else.

'You're very appreciative of beauty.' He turned to look down into her eyes. He was at her side and the subtle, elusive remnants of aftershave mingling with the odour of his body assailed her nostrils in pervasive heady waves. Nerve ends tingled, emotions heightened as the silent moments passed and she became more and more aware of him as a man—of his magnetic personality, the consummate power he had to arouse her senses, to fill her heart and mind with impossible desires.

She looked away, towards the harbour, where the inexpressible melding of colour and luminescence contributed even more atmosphere, adding to the magical impression of something out of a fairy tale. The water, crystal-bright, appeared smooth as silk, and argent in the moonglow.

It was far too romantic; her senses were alive to the nearness of Ramon, and she turned swiftly, deciding to escape to her bedroom. But, somehow, Ramon's foot seemed to get in her way and she jerked against him, the contact of his body an electric shock affecting her heartbeat. He caught and held her, the perfumed aureole of her hair tantalising against his face, his hands warm and strong on her arms. She quivered beneath his touch; his breath came warm against her cheeks. The glimmer of a smile touched his lips before, without Paula even suspecting his intention, he bent his head and she felt the nerve-tingling pressure of his lips on hers, sensuous, moist, possessive. He was crushing her against him; instinctively she struggled but found her hands caught in a grip of steel, and held behind her back. Then the instinct to struggle was lost in the desire to know more about him, his arrogant, domineering way with women. His eyes were dark, the fire within burning into hers; she could only stare up at him, drawn by the power he possessed. Her heart raced as his ardour increased; she tried desperately to use her common sense to control her thoughts so the consequences of this folly could be assessed, but the desire of the moment was paramount, the primordial yearning of the flesh, all powerful, irresistible. His mouth was hard against her softly yielding lips; she knew the thrill of his tongue sliding moistly over hers, then later finding her throat and a hypersensitive spot behind her ear. Her fingers caressed instinctively, touching his nape, sending vibrations through his body at the contact. She felt him quiver at the warm symmetry of her body and she arched it to his, and a little moan of pleasure escaped her as she savoured the force of his passion.

Presently he held her from him and she waited in agonised silence for him to make some half-sneering remark or, at best, to treat her with a sort of contemptuous, sardonic amusement. Instead, he looked deeply into her eyes and said, 'My dear, you act as if you love me.'

'I . . .' Her voice trailed as colour ebbed from her cheeks.

'Ought I to apologise?' And, when she did not answer, 'I don't intend to, Paula, because it was very plain that you wanted me to kiss you, just as much as I wanted to kiss you.' She still made no response and he added, 'I've wanted to kiss you, Paula, since the moment I set eyes on you.'

She shook her head in a swift and negative gesture.

'No, you couldn't have,' she protested, a trifle

dazed by his admission. 'You didn't even notice me as a woman.'

His hands were gentle as they enclosed her face.

'Come,' he said abruptly, 'it's time we were sleeping.'

Paula awoke the following morning to the awareness of sunshine filtering the shutters and she sat up, memory flooding over her, bringing colour to her cheeks and the recollection to her mind of the warning she had received from the woman who had interviewed her for the post of secretary to Ramon Calzada. Don't fall in love with him. Well, not only had she fallen in love with him but she had allowed him to see it. What further folly could she have committed? And now she must leave his employ and begin all over again, trying to mend her life . . . and her heart.

She felt she could not face him at the breakfast table, but of course there was no way of avoiding the meeting. And so she put on as casual an air as she could, entering the elegant room quietly and managing to produce a smile as she said with a slight nod of her head, 'Good morning, senor. I hope I haven't kept you waiting?'

'Not at all. Sit down, Paula—' He drew out a chair for her. 'Did you sleep well?'

She stared at him, staggered by the difference in his attitude towards her and by the total absence of any sign of contempt. Yet surely he must be thinking of all those other secretaries who had proved to be nuisances by falling in love with him. Surely he was now putting her into the same category and considering dismissing her from his service.

'Yes, very well, thank you, senor.'

Faintly he smiled, his eyes staring directly into hers.

'You're shy. I believe I remarked on the fact before. I find it rather refreshing to discover a woman who is shy.'

She looked down at her empty plate for a moment and then, 'I don't understand you, senor.'

To her surprise he laughed. Her breath caught at the sheer perfection of his features, at the flash of perfect white teeth, the creation of crinkly lines fanning out from the corners of his eyes. He could be devastating if only he were to forget those women who had let him down, and all the others whose favours he had enjoyed. Yes, if he could forget the past and fall in love. . . . Perhaps one day he would. Paula felt physically sick at the idea of some lucky woman winning him for a husband and in her heart the pain was almost physical. Well, should that happen, which after some consideration she felt was most unlikely, she would not be around to suffer. In fact, she would not be around much longer at all.

At the end of the week she would give him her notice.

The following evening he was charm itself, and Paula did not know when she had enjoyed a meal as much as the intimate, candlelit dinner set out for them on the pool patio where lights shone in the trees and on the pool—amber and rose and subtle peach. It was a romantic, friendly occasion and when at the end Ramon again took her in his arms and kissed her it seemed the most natural thing in the world for her to reciprocate. Yet the moment she had left him she was filled with shame and dread—yes, dread of the future, for she could see no real happiness for her for a very long time to come. Her logical mind assured her that she would eventually come to discover that the pain was not so acute; from then on it would become less and less noticeable until it was gone altogether. But the scar would remain, a reminder of her folly, and a barrier to perfect happiness with any other man.

The following evening Ramon took her to a mountain restaurant where they dined in a rustic atmosphere. There was a combo band, and after the first course of fried oysters, Ramon invited Paula to dance. She rose nervously, her mind still in a whirl of unreality at this staggering change in her employer's attitude towards her. She quivered beneath his touch as he slid an arm around her slender waist, and savoured the cool contact of his hand enclosing hers. She danced on air, losing her nervousness as she matched his expert steps—surprisingly without effort. Her confidence began to rise and she was able to look up into his face and talk to him as they danced.

'That was a real pleasure,' was his flattering comment as they resumed their places at the table. 'You dance very well, Paula.'

Paula. . . . He had used her Christian name ever since the night of the dinner with his client

Luis Perez. She felt her pulse race; her mind was in a daze by the unmistakable affection he was showing her.

Again when they arrived back at the Casa Don Felipe, Ramon took her in his arms and kissed her, and although fully aware that she was playing with fire, subjecting her heart to future pain, she decided it was worth it! The time was *now* and this was living! She was deliriously happy, living joyously for each and every moment without thought or care for the nebulous void that was the future, and which lay round a bend in life's road where the sun would be shut out for a very long while. But for the present, the sun was warm and bright in a sky of cloudless blue.

Chapter Four

The moon was brilliant on the shimmering sea,
the sky filled with stars—millions of them set in
a bed of purple velvet that trailed off into the
realms of eternity. So vast the arc of the heavens, and frightening!

Paula stood on the verandah of the Hacienda
Calzada waiting for Ramon to appear. She had
watched the sleekly-blended colours of sunset—
golds and russets, pink and coral—dissolve into
a sky of deepest purple. The emerald hills had
darkened before her eyes; the moon had risen to
become enormous; Paula had traced its argent
path across the glittering sea to where it sprayed
silver on the deserted beach which, in the glaze
of the mid-day sun, was dazzling white. She and
Ramon had been swimming in the afternoon,
then strolled along the shore. She had enjoyed
the gentle resilience of sand between her toes,
the sun's warmth on her near naked body. She
had watched with the first indefinable hint of
brooding his eyes devour the contours of her
figure, resting on places that brought colour to

her cheeks. He had looked his fill, over and over again and as on that first day she had felt like a piece of merchandise being examined for possible flaws before purchase. But she intended to take her pleasure while it lasted, playing with fire, subjecting her heart to excruciating pain in the future when Ramon, having enjoyed this affair with her, would cast her off, as he had cast off so many others who had come before her, and as he would do over and over again in the future.

He came silently up behind her, his hands came beneath her arms to cup her breasts. She turned to face him. His hand beneath her chin tilted it; she stood, quivering at his nearness, her lovely eyes large and pleading, pleading for something more than a mere affair, even while her heart and mind accepted that she had no future with this man whose only interest was in her body, and the pleasure he felt confident he would derive from it. His kiss was the pleasure-pain of temptation, his hands roved, fingers pressing her waist, finding vulnerable places that brought vibrations to her body as if from an electric shock. She made no demure when his hand slipped into the low neckline of her dress to cup one firm high breast within its warmth. Her whole frame quivered as she felt the moving warmth of his other hand stealing down to the lower part of her body, its pressure bringing her to him.

'You're . . . beautiful!' he whispered in a throaty bass tone. 'I want you, Paula; you must know how much I want you?' He held her from him, looked into eyes dreamy and glazed with desire and a laugh escaped him. 'You want me—say it,' he commanded. 'Don't you dare deny it, Paula!'

Vaguely she wondered if any woman had denied it, when brought almost to surrender by the incredible finesse of his technique.

'No,' she whispered, resting her head against his chest and putting an arm around his neck. 'No, Ramon, I couldn't deny it. You see—' The rest was smothered by his passionate kisses, and her body was swept into a maelstrom of passion she would never have believed possible. No wonder the Latin American man was notorious for his passionate nature.

'Let us go and have dinner,' he said at last, his breathing heavy and erratic. 'No, we must wait a few moments, mustn't we?' His hand was gentle as he touched her hair, putting unruly strands into place, or trying to.

'I'll go and comb it,' she smiled. 'Shall I come back here?'

'No, I shall be in the dining-room.'

Much later they were walking in the garden, and as Paula expected, Ramon stopped in a secluded spot and took her in his arms. Her hands curled against his chest, as if instinctively she would push him away. Yet she was already halfway to surrender, yearning for his lips on hers, his long brown fingers caressing her curves. She could sense the latent force of his passion as he seemed to sway, trapped in the yearning eagerness of her desires, portrayed unashamedly in the arch of her slim young body, the rapt expression in her eyes.

'I want you, Paula. . . .' Briefly he held her from him.

She said nothing. She was drawn into his arms, the impact with his hard, virile body temptation in itself. The pressure of his demanding mouth sent feathery tingles of ecstasy quivering along her spine. Her heart was beating overrate and she knew he must be aware of her heightened emotions. His tongue with determined insistence forced her lips apart and the heady sensation of his exploration into her mouth added fuel to the fire of her longing for him . . . for moments of bliss . . . and of folly.

'Paula,' he whispered huskily, 'you're the most desirable woman I have ever met. What is it about you that is different?'

The words which ought to have brought joy, chilled her instead. She leant away from him and words she did not mean to utter left her quivering lips.

'You've had dozens of women?'

'I've had a few,' he answered her casually.

'And now you want me?'

'More than any of the others.'

'How long does an affair usually last with you?'

His mouth twisted contemptuously.

'Until I tire. I find women so very temperamental. They start off resigned to an affair that will end with the inevitable "goodbye, it was nice while it lasted," but then they suddenly decide they want permanency—they want marriage.' He gave a hard laugh, his eyes narrowed and contemptuous. 'Do they suppose a man will accept marriage when he can get all he wants—and plenty of variety—without the obligations which marriage inevitably brings?'

Paula moved out of his arms and away from

him. Her face was pale, her mouth twisting convulsively. All the new-born love rose like a floodtide within her and she knew she would let him have an affair with her. Love was like that; it craved fulfilment, and despite the knowledge of a future where regrets must inevitably invade her mind, she desired only to live for the present, to savour the caresses, the expert lovemaking of this distinguished man into whose life she had been catapulted by the caprice of fate.

'You—want me?' she said again, in a faltering voice.

'I want you, yes,' he replied matter-of-factly. She was a small distance from him and he pointed, indicating a spot close to where he was standing. 'Come here,' he ordered, and without a pause she found herself obeying. The dark Spanish eyes were unfathomable as he took her in his arms, tilting her chin as his head came down towards her face. She felt the demanding pressure of his lips, the caress of his exploring hands and every nerve-cell in her body responded, passion rocking her like the force of a storm, while Ramon's rising ardour manifested itself in the urgency of his breathing, the more determined exploration of his hands as they caressed her curves. 'How delightful you are,' he murmured, the feather touch of his lips against her throat. She heard a soft laugh of triumph as the whole yielding length of her body was pressed against him, conveying her need in every sigh and gesture. It was inevitable that she be swept into the fiery torrent of his lovemaking, and as the minutes passed the desire for the supreme joy became torment. She waited, breathless from the forceful demands of his mouth, for him

to make the decision. Vaguely she wondered
whether they would sleep in her room or his—

She cut her thoughts, for the whole idea
seemed crude, suddenly. To indulge in an affair
with a man she had known until very recently as
her employer, who by his own admission considered women as mere playthings, unworthy of
any sensitive consideration. This was the man
with whom she was contemplating an affair.
Filled with disgust that almost reached nauseat-
ing proportions, she broke from him, faced him
and said fiercely, 'I'm not having an affair with
you, Senor Calzada! Yes, I know what you are
going to say—that I was willing just now. You
must know of your attraction for women and I
was—was carried away, but my commonsense
came to my rescue, thank God! And now,' she
added, glowering at him, 'there remains only for
me to give you my notice. I shall be leaving in a
month's time!'

'I might eventually accept your notice. As for
there remaining *only* for you to give me your
notice—you're mistaken, my dear. It remains
only for me to ask you to be my wife.'

Paula had turned away but at his words she
spun around, her eyes dilating, her heart giving
a great lurch that set it throbbing against her
ribs.

'Wh-what d-did you say?' she stammered, sure
she had not heard correctly. 'I th-thought . . .'
Her voice trailed to silence as she spread her
hands helplessly. For there was no expression on
his face; *it might have been a mask of stone*,
she thought.

'I asked you to marry me,' he told her unemo-
tionally. He seemed a long way from her, his

eyes brooding, his lips tight. What was his objective in talking like this? He was not serious. How could he be?

'Is this some kind of a joke?' managed Paula at last. 'If so, then I don't think much of your sense of humour.' Her chin lifted automatically and a sparkle lit her eyes. 'You've just said you don't want marriage because you can get all you want without it—and you can have variety—' She stopped, colour fusing her face. She hadn't meant to add that little bit at all.

'I was referring to other women, not you. It isn't a joke, Paula,' he added seriously, and she caught the conviction in his words. 'I've found you so different from any other woman I have ever known, that I want you for my wife.' He paused a moment to give her the chance to speak. When she remained silent he added softly, 'Haven't I already told you that you are very different from the rest?'

'Yes, but—' She shook her head in bewilderment, searching for words of eloquence that would be fitting to a situation like this but merely coming out with, 'You aren't the marrying kind, senor,' and instantly feeling extremely foolish, especially on noticing the glimmer of amusement that had entered his eyes.

'I certainly wasn't the marrying kind until you came into my life,' he readily admitted. 'But now—' He spread his hands expressively. 'Now, my dear, I feel it's time I married. I want to settle down, with you.'

She looked at him, endeavouring to read his thoughts. Her heart should by rights have been bounding with joy; she should be asking herself how this miracle had happened. But there was within her a sort of numb disquietude, a tingling, nervous reaction, not only to the unbelievable words he had uttered, but to his manner as well.

It was scarcely that of a lover, an ardent suitor whose only desire in life was to win her for his own.

From the recesses of her mind there emerged the logical answer to give him, but although determination lit her eyes, there was a certain hesitancy in her voice as she said, 'I can't marry you, senor. It—it just wouldn't work.'

Reaching out, he brought her unresistingly into his arms. He bent his head and she could not help the thrill that rippled through her at the contact of his lips with hers. He kissed her passionately, finding sensitive places on her throat and behind her ear. She clung to him, wanting nothing more than to be like this, in his arms. . . . What foolishness when she had just declined to marry him! Where was her strength, her commonsense?

'You're afraid,' he murmured gently, his moist lips caressing her cheek. 'It came as a surprise, didn't it? And yet surely you could see that I was attracted?' She shook her head but he went on, ignoring the gesture, 'I know that you love me, Paula. You've revealed it to me more than once.'

She could not deny it and she found herself nodding in instant agreement, then she coloured up and once again caught a glimmer of amusement in his eyes.

'I d-don't know what to say,' she quivered, feeling all at once that this must be a dream, not really happening—just something born of her yearning for him, and the love she had unwillingly given him.

He kissed her gently on the lips and said, 'Just say yes, my dear, and we shall both be happy.'

She leant away from him and shook her head. She was fighting desperately . . . but her heart was weak and yielding. She wanted him so, craved to be his wife, to have him possess her, body and soul. She could picture the future as a pathway spread with rose petals . . . if only Ramon had been as perfect in character as he was in looks and physique. But he was a rake, and she could visualise heartache and disillusionment in plenty when, the novelty having worn off, he would carelessly turn to another woman, and then another, and it would go on like that, with his regretting the weak moment when he had asked Paula to marry him.

'Ramon—senor—'

'Ramon will do, my dear,' he assured her, smiling down into her pale, strained countenance. 'Paula, you want to marry me, so why are you hesitating?'

She tried to answer, to explain what was in her mind—the fears and doubts, the distrust which she hated to admit was there. But he was looking tenderly at her, and there was anxiety in his expression too, and she felt herself quite unable to confess what was in her mind.

'It's come as—as such a shock,' she quavered, a tiny sob escaping her unintentionally. She had no idea just how helpless she appeared to him, how vulnerable and unsure of herself. Her lovely eyes were unconsciously pleading; she had no idea that she was begging for some sign that he loved her, that his wish to marry her was more than mere desire for her body. Vaguely she had supposed it *was* desire for her body that had prompted his action, and yet at the same time there was the sure conviction that he was fully aware that he could have her without very much effort at all.

So why did he want to marry her? Paula's mind was so confused that she felt she wanted to cry, to go away and be quiet . . . and unhappy, on her own.

'Naturally it was a surprise,' he agreed, 'but as for its being a shock—well, as I have just said, you must have realised that I was finding you attractive?'

'I believed it was only physically,' Paula found herself admitting.

'I could not deny that, my dear,' he returned with a smile. His hands tightened on her arms, and he bent his head to take her softly-parted lips in a kiss that was as ardent as it was tender. 'I want you physically, just as you want me. But also I want to settle down and have a family. A man tires of the insecure life eventually.'

She said, looking directly into his eyes, 'You haven't said you love me.'

The merest hesitation and then, 'Dear Paula, I thought you would take that for granted. Why else would I want to marry you?' He was shaking his head in a gesture of admonishment. 'Silly child—of course I love you.'

Her lips quivered then parted in a smile. Suddenly her heart was light, her fears completely eroded by the words he had uttered so sincerely. What was the matter with her that she had not realised he must love her? Otherwise he would never have dreamed of asking her to marry him.

Her smile deepened, and all the love she felt for him was in her eyes as she said, with a sort of shy hesitancy, 'I'll marry you, Ramon, and oh, but I'm so happy!'

'And you have made me happy, too, my darling.' She was swept passionately into his arms, her whole mind and heart carried away by what was happening to her. His kisses were soon firing her blood; she clung to him, straining her slender body, thrilling to the feel of his. She wondered if he was conscious of the wild, uncontrolled beating of her heart.

'You'll marry me soon,' he said in a throaty bass voice, and she answered him at once, saying yes, at any time he liked. Nevertheless, she drew away with an exclamation of protest and disbelief when he said, 'In three or four days then. There isn't anything for us to wait for.'

'Three or four days,' she echoed. 'But, Ramon, that doesn't give us any time at all!'

'What time do we want?' he inquired softly. 'We obviously can't have a big wedding. You have no one to invite and as for me—well, my friends would never expect me to enter into any fuss.'

'You mean,' she faltered, 'that we're not having a—a party?'

His swift laugh was tender; it never occurred to Paula that it was deliberately meant to be reassuring.

'Why should we care about a party? What we're doing, my darling, concerns us. Do you think I can contain my patience much longer? I want you, my love—now, if that were possible!'

Flattering words that swept away any further
protest she might have made. She was on air
that he wanted her so much he could not wait
more than three or four days. And as she examined her own feelings she found herself admitting unashamedly that any wait would prove to
be a strain. In spite of all this, though, she could
not stem the little access of regret and sense of
loss at their not having that precious interlude of
courtship that would have given them the opportunity of learning more about each other.

Ramon was speaking again, saying that the
ceremony would be in the private chapel, here,
on the estate, and the witnesses would be two
trusted servants who had been with him many
years, and with his father before him. Paula
listened, and felt a tinge of sadness that her
mother would not be here. But even had Ramon agreed to wait, Paula felt sure her mother
would not go to the trouble of coming all this
way to attend her daughter's wedding. Paula's
thoughts naturally went to Denis for a moment;
she would have to write to him, and at once, she
decided, fervently hoping that, if there was a
letter on its way from him, it would not contain
anything about their becoming engaged.

'My dress, Ramon,' she said presently, her
thoughts drifting from the mundane to the
magic. 'Where shall I get it—in such a short
time, I mean? There won't be time to have it
made.'

'There are several excellent boutiques in town
where you'll be able to get all you want.' He
paused a moment, smiling down into her
flushed and happy face. 'If you need any money,
dear, just ask for it.'

She made no answer; she was thinking of girlhood dreams of ivory satin and lace, of orange blossom and bouquets . . . and of a reception for a hundred guests. . . .

And instead of all that she was to be married in a ready-made dress from a boutique in town, married quietly without even one bridesmaid, without one present, one guest. A sigh escaped her.

'What is it, Paula?' Ramon's soft and gentle voice recalled her and she managed a smile. And then, impulsively, she put her arms around his neck and buried her face in his chest.

'It's n-nothing,' she replied in a muffled voice when he had repeated his question, 'nothing at all.'

'You're happy?'

'Of course.' And she knew she spoke the truth. 'I was just a little regretful that I'd have no one of my own at the wedding. Mother wouldn't have come anyway, and as for friends . . . well, it would have been nice to have one or two, but as it isn't possible it's profitless to let it trouble me.'

'You're a sensible girl,' he approved, *and his voice did seem to have a casual, indifferent edge to it*, she thought, but the idea dissolved when, with a sudden smile, Ramon kissed her tenderly on the lips.

Chapter Five

They had been married less than a week when Paula felt the first tinge of uneasiness assail her. It was no more than a frail thread, almost nebulous. Certainly it was nothing tangible which she could grasp, hold on to and analyse. Vaguely she wondered if it were the speed with which Ramon had wanted to be married. His excuse was acceptable enough; she had been flattered by his impatience, by his ardent desire to possess her. Yet she had begun to feel instinctively that there was something inexplicable about the whole procedure of their marriage, but it was impossible to find out anything because there was never an occasion where her husband's manner invited questions. On one occasion it had even occurred to her that he might have some ulterior motive for marrying her, but such an idea had been instantly thrust out of her mind, since she could not possibly substantiate it.

As for Ramon's attitude towards her, it was without fault. He was kind, considerate and loving. He had voluntarily offered information about himself—after asking her to tell her story first.

'I've told you most of it,' she had said. 'My parents got a divorce. . . .' She had continued, telling him of her life after that upheaval, and ending by mentioning Denis with whom she had been keeping company for the six months prior to his taking the post on the cruise ship. 'We never had any definite understanding,' she added finally.

'So that is all?' he had asked, watching her seriously.

'Yes, that is all. Nothing exciting ever happened to me until now.' Her smile was loving, her glance tender. Ramon had looked away as he began to talk about his family. Paula, listening with keen interest, learned of the infidelity of his father, and the instant reaction of his mother who believed in an eye for an eye, and promptly found herself a lover whom she flaunted in her errant husband's face whenever the opportunity presented itself. And as Ramon proceeded it was not difficult for Paula to form an accurate picture of his unhappiness, for she had undergone similar suffering herself. Ramon had clung to his elder sister, his only anchor in the storm-tossed atmosphere of insecurity that resulted from the selfishness and neglect of his parents. Then his sister suddenly deserted him, running off one night, leaving a short note to say she could no longer stay in a home that was breaking up. She was going to New York to live with a friend, and there she intended to find work and make a new life for herself. Ramon at that time was only thirteen years of age; he continued at

school but within a year another upheaval occurred in his life; his parents separated and he
was placed in a boarding school and left there,
even during the holidays.

'Your misfortunes are similar to mine in a
way,' commented Paula, when a lapse occurred
in his narrative, 'but yours were far more severe
than mine. I had a friend and her mother was
exceedingly good to me at that time. I felt I could
lean on her, and I often did.'

Ramon had nodded absently and she rather
thought he had not paid much attention to what
she had been saying.

'I went in for law, and that part of my life was
a success,' he continued, his manner remote, his
expression distant. 'I have never seen my sister
from that day to this,' he informed Paula bitterly, digressing from the main theme of the story
for a moment. 'We were very close and devoted
before she went away, and yet she never com-
municated. It seems unbelievable even now.'

'Perhaps something happened to her,' suggested Paula.

He shook his head.

'She's alive, and happily married. I spoke to
someone a few weeks ago who had attended a
wedding to which she and her husband had been
invited.' An interval of silence followed and
Paula leant back in her chair, her ears attuned
to the symphony of tumbling water as it cascaded down from the fountain outside the room in
which she and Ramon were sitting. 'I became
engaged,' she heard him say after a while, and
his dark eyes were brooding as if memories tore
at his heart. 'I had faith in her, and in our life
together but—' He stopped abruptly and once

more silence reigned between them. 'I was not very well off in those days—my father owned this estate and I believed he would leave it to my sister, as she was always his favourite. I was making my way as a lawyer, but on the whole I had little to offer a wife . . . except love. . . .' He drifted away, into the past, and something had turned in Paula's heart, something painful which she thought was for Ramon's hurt, but yet she wondered if it were for her own. 'She accepted me and seemed happy enough, but then she jilted me for a man she went to work for; he was extremely wealthy.' He stopped, the brooding expression on his face more pronounced than ever. Paula's nerves had become taut; she felt a sort of breathless pain, as if something had frightened her momentarily and the result was physical. But the sensation passed and she was saying with a tender smile, 'Your experiences made you bitter, but it's all over now, darling. You and I will have a wonderful life together.'

He had nodded and reached for her hand; she thrilled to the warmth and strength of his fingers, to the movement of his thumb sliding over the soft smooth skin of her palm.

'Yes, we shall have a good life together,' he had agreed, but suddenly he was not looking at her but through her, as if it were a very different picture that was focused within his mental vision.

Noticing nothing unusual, Paula had lapsed into a contented silence, dwelling for a space on his unfortunate experiences with the three women who had let him down. Well, his wife would never let him down; her love was deep and strong, yet she knew it would become stronger and stronger with every year that passed.

Her thoughts returned to the uneasiness she had begun to feel, but it was unprofitable because she had nothing to put her finger on. And so she relived her wedding day, as she had relived it several times during the past week.

'You look so beautiful,' Magdalena had said when Paula, almost ready, stood regarding herself critically in the long, gilt-framed mirror. She had been very lucky in her purchases, managing to find a calf-length dress of wild silk designed in Edwardian style with a high neckline and long full sleeves gathered into a cuff trimmed with delicate lace matching the lace on the collar and along the edge of the hem. Her accessories were of coral pink, the hat most becoming with its very wide brim and ribbons hanging down the back. 'I never thought that Senor Calzada would ever get married,' Magdalena could not help saying. 'Everybody will be very surprised.'

Paula had smiled, and being all woman it was inevitable that she should dwell a little triumphantly on what all Ramon's ex-girlfriends would think on hearing he was married and no longer free to engage in affairs with them.

The actual ceremony had been swift, yet it was a solemn occasion, and when it was over Ramon took his bride in his arms and kissed her tenderly.

'You're so beautiful,' he whispered, and because his words were music in her ears she was able to cast off any small access of regret at not having the kind of wedding she had always visualised.

Much later, wearing a Paris-made evening dress of midnight blue organza, Paula stood with her husband on the terrace of the hacienda, her hand in his, her head against his shoulder. They had dined at home, in an atmosphere of candleglow and flowers, of antique silver and cut glass, had eaten superb food and drunk fine vintage wine, while chatting and listening to soft music to which they danced between the courses. It had been a time of sheer enchantment for Paula, whose cup of happiness was full to overflowing. And now, she and Ramon were enjoying a few minutes outside where, in the near distance, moonbeams were painting silver ribbons on the sea. Absorbed in the incredible, inescapable beauty of the landscape, Paula felt she was floating on the wings of a dream, with reality a nebulous quality existing somewhere a million miles away. Earlier in the afternoon she had stood here alone, while Ramon made some important telephone calls; she had seen the gentle slopes reflecting the sapphire blues of sea and sky, had watched the wavelets caress the palm-fringed beach to create a magical blending of shape and colour. She had stood in awed wonderment, staring down at the fantastic coral formations looming pink and green beneath the crystal-clear water of the lagoon.

And now the whole delightful spectrum of colour and sound and smells had changed, and it was the moon's argent glow that painted everything, transforming the emerald hills to silver, the frothing wavelets to purest white.

Paula leant against her husband, deliberately tempting him; his arm came about her waist, his lips finding a tender place along the curve of her throat. He kissed her, his sensuous lips moist and hot against the coolness of hers. His tongue caressed, tantalising deliberately and Ramon laughed softly on feeling her body quiver against him.

'Let's go in,' he said softly. 'I can't wait any longer for you . . . my lovely wife.'

There were two bedrooms in the suite, and two bathrooms. In one room there was a king-size bed—enormous—of the kind Paula had never seen before.

'The Americans usually have king-size beds,' Ramon had explained earlier, 'and these beds were bought in the States.'

So many things came from the States, Paula had discovered, but then, Puerto Rico was an American island.

'But we still retain our Latin American personality,' Ramon had been swift to assure her.

He had entered the bedroom behind her and closed the door with a quiet click. Paula swung round lightly, her dress flowing about her feet like that of a dancer. Ramon stood motionless, his eyes, dark and piercing, seemed for a fleeting moment to brood, and to stare beyond her as if he were looking for another picture to become focused within his vision. The atmosphere became electric; she whispered huskily, 'Ramon . . . what is it?' and the next moment he was smiling.

'My wife,' he murmured. 'How very tempting you are.'

He was dynamic, just as Paula had known he

would be, with that Latin American temperament of his and the innate sense of mastery which was also a part of him. She steeled herself for the kind of lovemaking that not one in a hundred Englishmen would understand. She tingled in every expectant nerve as he moved gracefully towards her with lithe unhurried steps. She was vitally conscious of the languid, latent power that his body movements portrayed. There was arrogance in every step he took, all the inbred superiority of his Spanish ancestors. Like them, he would take just whenever he chose to do so, and in his own dominating way.

She was standing with her back to the window, moonglow behind her, a rapt expression on her face, her big eyes limpid pools of happiness. He was hers!—this superlative man who had chosen her from all other women he had known!

He stopped; she waited for the order that would bid her to go to him.

'Come here.' So soft the words, but authoritative, and his eyes, unwavering on her face, clearly reflected the command in his voice.

She obeyed, with steps that faltered in spite of her eagerness to be in his arms. Reaching out, he drew her possessively towards him, lean brown fingers immediately tracing a line along her cheek to the curves of her throat and shoulder. She looked up into his dark face, searching for an expression of love, but his eyes were unfathomable, his lips curved in a twisted, lingering smile. Paula could only stare mutely, wondering at his thoughts and feeling almost shut out . . . someone who was suddenly in the way!

He looked down at her at last, his expression veiled still, but the twisted smile was gone and he seemed to be coming back to her. Within moments she had forgotten everything but the thrill of his kiss, the pleasurable pain of his crushing embrace. Her sensitive nostrils became profoundly affected by the aroma of his body, mingling with the fresh wild heather of after shave and the result was magnetic, drawing her to him, stripping her of all reserve. Unashamedly she arched her slender body in seductive sensuality, allowing her arms to creep up around his neck, then wander to his nape and into his hair.

'You're incredibly tempting! Paula, you're so alive!' He wasted no time in dealing with the zipper of her dress, and she blushed adorably as its folds swirled downwards, to settle around her feet. Her bra was removed next and she was held at a distance so that he could take his fill of her near-naked body. Something more than passion stirred her senses. . . . She was seeing him with other women, his almost lecherous gaze devouring their smooth-skinned beauty, and in his dark foreign eyes the shades of contempt. Her eyes lifted; she half-expected to see a scornful expression on his face, but what she did encounter was deep admiration. And yet almost immediately his expression changed and she could read nothing from the chiselled mask he had drawn over his face. Incomprehensible, with a shield around him still. . . . But no. How could her thoughts be wandering on lines like that? She was facing the most wonderful moment of her life, for whatever came afterwards there would never be another night quite like their wedding night.

His hands were sliding over her body, warm and strong and very reassuring. Ecstasy swept through her as her blood was set on fire by the masterful provocation of his touch on her breast. His lips roved in sensual exploration to rest eventually against the ivory curve above his hand.

'You're . . . delectable!' Ramon's voice was hoarse, throaty, deepened by passion. 'I've never known seductiveness like this before. I always believed Englishwomen were cold, and even unapproachable when they chose to be perverse, but you . . . my beautiful, reciprocal wife—' His words shuddered to a stop as, having unbuttoned his shirt, Paula slid her hands against his ribcage. His body quivered against the yielding softness of her curves, and when, a moment later, she felt the hardening peaks of her breasts imprisoned in his long, sensitive fingers, the sensual abandon of her own desire was the flame to ignite the ardour already smouldering within him. A vein throbbed in his temple; his gaze moved to the gentle swell of her throat, then lower to the delightful lobes of her breasts, and with a wild, primitive motion he swept her into his arms, strode to the bed and laid her down. Her long lashes fluttered, for she was too shy to watch him undress. She heard the rustle of clothes, imagining him taking off his garments one by one. And then he was beside her; she knew the redolence of her flesh against his, knew the agony of desire stabbing through her loins; she gasped in the throes of ecstasy as one vibration after another racked her body as her husband swept her into the vortex of his primitive, unleashed ardour.

The week following their wedding had been a time of bliss for Paula, with her husband giving her all she could ever have wanted, both mentally and physically. They were attuned in matters of art and music, and of the appreciation of nature in all its aspects. She and Ramon had spent a little time on the beach during the first two days, with Ramon doing some underwater exploration. The following day he had taken her to Parguera, a pretty fishing village where they had eaten grilled lobster for lunch before setting off in a motor boat to tour the bay. Ramon had insisted they stay until dark so that Paula could witness the strange phenomenon of the bright green sparks flashing through the water of Phosphorescent Bay. He told Paula to draw her arm through the water, which she did, and exclaimed in wonderment and delight when a great arc of quicksilver flashes appeared.

They left the hacienda for Old San Juan four days after the wedding, but Paula did not mind in the least because she had many ideas for changes she wanted to make at the Casa Don Felipe. Not that she had any intention of changing the general atmosphere in any way, on the contrary, she was delighted with the shady patios glimpsed through leafy arches, the terraced garden—not nearly so grand as that of the hacienda, but delightful in a very different way—the ancient, intricate wrought-iron balconies . . . all these retained the flavour of old Spain, of the Spanish Grandees in their opulent prime, and to wander about among them was an experience of which Paula knew she would never tire. But the interior of the casa was in part somewhat severe, and she began to add a tapestry here and there, which she discovered in the attic rooms, secreted away in ancient wooden trunks and now brought to light again. She fetched rugs from little used rooms to adorn the marble floor of the dining room; she moved chairs and couches, added paintings and ornaments, side-tables and cushions.

Her efforts brought a flattering observation from her husband.

'It's beginning to look more like home every day. You're a marvel, especially as you are still working at the office.'

Paula laughed and was happy, basking in the rosy glow of his approval. All she wished was to serve him, to do whatever she could to make his life perfect in every way. Never could she have visualised loving like this; it was a soul-sweeping experience and she often felt herself floating, as if she were in the realms of heaven itself.

'I'm so happy I'm frightened,' she confessed to Ramon one evening when they had returned to the house after a very busy day at the office. 'Who am I to be as lucky as this?'

To her astonishment he uttered no words of reassurance, made no move to take her in his arms and kiss away her fears. Instead, he turned slightly from her and she suspected the action was made so that his expression would be hidden from her. She fell silent, staring at the aperitif Ramon had poured for her and which stood on a side-table at her elbow. She and

Ramon had not changed yet, and she was in a pastel green summer dress, low-cut and sleeveless. She crossed her shapely legs and leant back in the chair, her eyes now focused on her husband who had not yet turned to look at her.

What was the matter? Until now the only shadow on her horizon was that she would have had her husband a little more demonstrative, and yet she was at the same time accepting that, when she first knew him, she had been convinced that he was too cold and distant ever to be demonstrative, too self-contained ever to allow emotions—other than sexual ones—to come to the surface.

Again she was conscious of a thread of doubt, and now she began to wonder if it had been there all the time, and that she had automatically thrown it off, continuing to live in paradise, with the hours and days flying by on golden wings.

'Is something wrong?' she asked at last and Ramon turned then, and she noticed the brooding expression in his eyes.

He shook his head absently.

'No—what could be wrong?'

'You're not the same,' she faltered, an unconscious catch in her voice. 'You seem to be—er—sad. . . .'

He stared at her, then shook his head again.

'Darling,' he chided, 'why should I be sad when I have a wonderful wife like you?'

Her world was rosy again; she went to him, put her arms about his neck and lifted her face for his kiss.

'I love you, Ramon,' she whispered huskily when he had kissed her. 'I love you so much that it hurts.'

He seemed to utter a little sigh of impatience, and a frown creased Paula's wide forehead. But as she lifted her face to look into his eyes she saw nothing to alarm her and she decided she had been imagining things. He bent to kiss her, and his arms were strong and reassuring about her. She was foolish and fanciful, she admonished herself later. If she wasn't very careful, she'd become a clinging wife whose continual need for demonstrations of love from her husband would very soon begin to pall, especially with a man like Ramon.

She resolved to be a little less emotional in future.

Chapter Six

It was five days later that Ramon told Paula he would be away from home and the office for a couple of days.

'I have to see a client who's a cripple,' he went on. 'He lives here, in San Juan, normally, but at present he's with his sister in Haiti. It's imperative that I see him, and it'll mean my staying overnight because there's rather a lot to discuss.'

'You don't need me with you?' the plea in her voice either went unnoticed or was deliberately ignored.

'You're needed in the office. There will be the phone to answer, and many of the calls will be important. There are letters, too, which I have already dictated to you.'

She nodded, feeling flat, and instantly admonished herself for it. After all, it would be less than two days that her husband would be away.

She wanted to drive him to the airport, just to be with him until the last moment; and she would also be able to meet him on his return the following day, but he would not hear of it. He would drive himself, he said, and leave the car at the airport overnight.

After his departure at lunch time, Paula busied herself until the usual time of five o'clock, when she closed the office and strolled home through the narrow streets paved with the stone brought as ballast in the galleons of Spain. The sun was going down, and in the slanting rays she was able to appreciate more than ever the atmosphere of sixteenth- and seventeenth-century Spain portrayed in the lovely old buildings with their curious arched doorways, mellowed and peaceful in the afterglow of the swiftly-lowering sun. Sights, sounds and smells all contributed to the heady sensation of unreality—the perfume of frangipani, the scent of mango flowers in the gardens she was passing, the perfume of lemon blossom drifting on crystal-clear air from some unseen place. At the northwest tip of the city rose the massive fortress of El Morro, soaring to a hundred and fifty feet above the Atlantic. Impregnable bastion of colonial Spain, it had resisted the determined attacks of doughty Englishmen like Drake and Hawkins, who had failed to break through its fortifications.

At last Paula found herself coming from the darkening streets of the city into the lighted courtyard of the Casa Don Felipe. From the terraced garden drifted the perfume of flowers—tropical lilies and orchids and numerous exotic trees. She stood for a few moments savouring the atmosphere of peace as the garden became enveloped in the lovely blue-mauve afterglow of a Caribbean sunset.

The house seemed strangely deserted as she entered, in spite of the ready greeting of the housekeeper and the delicious smell of cooking.

It was strange, dining alone, and yet Paula could not help but recall how, until she had come to work for the man who was now her husband, she had eaten alone almost every night of her life.

After dinner she went up to the bedroom, found herself pacing aimlessly about from one side to the other and, giving herself a mental shake, she found a book of poems, took it out on to the balcony, and found a secluded corner sheltered by a beautiful bougainvillaea vine. After switching on the muted light above her head, she settled down to an interlude of quiet reading.

It must have been less than a quarter of an hour later that voices intruded into the incessant trilling of cicadas and, frowning in puzzlement, Paula automatically lowered her book to her knees. One voice was that of Adela, the housekeeper, the other that of a younger woman—an arrogant, imperative Spanish voice speaking in English. Rising stealthily, Paula traversed the balcony, which ran the full length of three bedrooms and over a leafy stone-flagged courtyard which was at right angles to the front façade of the house. The voices were quite clear from this point and without compunction Paula listened, intrigued by the imperious, demanding voice of the visitor.

'I don't believe he's away! I know you,

Adela—you dislike me and try to keep me from
your master! You did it three weeks ago, remember, and I believed you and went away. But
when I rang him the following day he said he
was in! Let me pass, at once!' She was speaking
in Spanish now but of course Paula could understand every word of what she was saying. Who
was she? And by what right was she able to
adopt this attitude with Ramon's highly-
respected servant? Ramon himself would never
have spoken to Adela in that particular tone of
voice.

'He is away,' came the housekeeper's raised
voice. She also spoke in Spanish and was answered even before the last syllable was out of
her mouth.

'You lie, Adela! And why are you acting so
strangely? You're furtive, glancing about you all
the time. This proves to me that your master is
in. He's in his study and I'd call if I thought he
could hear me. Announce me at once!'

'I can't announce you to someone who isn't
here, Senora Donado. Believe me, Senor
Calzada is not at home!' A fleeting silence
followed before the housekeeper added, unmistakable urgency in her voice, 'You *must* believe
me, and leave at once!'

'That is just it, I do not believe you.' Smooth
the tone all at once, but still commanding and
imperious. Who was this woman? Paula was
asking herself again, aware of her heart beating
rather quickly and of a tautness affecting her
nerves. 'It doesn't suit you for me to marry your
master, does it?' the voice went on, its sneering
quality lost on Paula as she took in the woman's

incredible words. 'You know I shall dismiss you at once, because of your persistent rudeness to me! I am not used to being treated so by mere servants! And now, woman, allow me to pass you. I shall see Ramon no matter what you say!'

'It doesn't suit you for me to marry your master. . . .' The words were still repeating themselves over and over again in Paula's brain, and she was aware of perspiration breaking out on her temples, and in the palms of her tightly-clenched hands. The woman was well-known to Adela, obviously, and it was also obvious that her position with Ramon had been such that she believed she had a chance of marrying him. Paula's mind recalled the name . . . Senora Donado . . . senora. The title of a married woman, Paula herself now being known as Senora Calzada. Paula's natural instinct was to move, to show herself, but some indefinable force held her back; she would listen for a little while longer.

'Go away, Miss Rosa—!' For some reason the housekeeper had broken into English, which she almost always used when speaking to Paula. 'Mrs. Rosa, I mean! It is not good that you stay, because I speak the truth when I tell you that Senor Calzada is not at home. He is in Haiti, with a client.'

A silence followed; Paula, nerves more erratic than ever, wished she could see the girl. From her voice she had gathered much about her personality, and now as her mind began to form pictures she saw her as an immaculately-attired woman carrying herself with total confidence and looking like something out of a glossy fashion magazine. Slinky, perhaps, and sexy,

with a figure to be envied . . . the sort of figure
that had attracted Ramon in the past.

'Stand aside!' came the insolent command at
last. 'I intend to enter this house!'

'Please. . . . Oh, Senora Rosa, you do not understand what has happened! I cannot let you
in—it's impossible!'

For some reason Adela had decided not to
inform the girl that Ramon was married and,
understanding her discomfort, Paula decided it
was time she showed herself. Speeding back
along the balcony, she entered the bedroom,
crossed it swiftly, and was soon descending the
balustraded staircase with the same quiet haste.
She saw the girl's eyes widen as she looked over
the broad shoulders of the housekeeper.

'Who—?'

'Oh, dear!' cried Adela, having turned her
head. There was an anxious, almost pained
expression on her face, noticed Paula. 'Senora,'
she began hesitantly, 'I'm sorry, but this lady
called to see—' She stopped, biting her lip and
glancing from one girl to the other. 'I tried to
make her go, because she has come to see Senor
Calzada, but she does not believe he is away
from home.' Again she stopped, anger darkening
her eyes as the visitor came past her into the hall
and was standing in an arrogant pose, looking at
Paula. In a fleeting but thorough glance Paula
had taken in the classic Spanish beauty of the
girl's features, the slender figure, the sleek black
hair above delicately-arched brows, the large
dark eyes, blue-shadowed and neatly lined. The
girl wore a perfectly-cut suit of light blue linen,
with shoes and handbag to match. In her ears
she wore heavy drops, and a matching bracelet

adorned her left wrist. A diamond and sapphire ring glittered on the third finger of her right hand; the fingers of her left hand bore no rings at all.

'Who is this person?' demanded Rosa, her eyes insolently raking Paula's body from head to foot. 'How does she come to be here . . . ?' Her voice trailed as enlightenment dawned. 'Ah . . . the English secretary Ramon mentioned to me. You live here, he was saying—'

'Can I ask who you are?' interrupted Paula, amazed at the steadiness of her voice when every nerve in her body was rioting.

'What has that to do with you?' the girl returned haughtily. 'Keep your place, girl! You're a servant; go back to your own quarters and mind your own business!'

Adela, deeply shocked, began to stammer in Spanish but Paula scarcely heard. It had struck her that this girl, Senora Donado, had accepted the fact that Ramon was not at home, since otherwise she would hardly be carrying on like this. Arrogant as Ramon was himself, Paula could not imagine his admiring arrogance in this visitor of his.

'I can manage this situation,' she found herself saying in an attempt to make the housekeeper feel more comfortable. 'You can go, Adela.'

Adela seemed a trifle reluctant, looking at Paula with concern, as if she were wondering if she needed support. At Paula's reassuring smile, however, she left the two girls alone, to stare at one another wordlessly for a moment, and it was Rosa who eventually broke the silence to ask,

'*Are* you Ramon's secretary?' with an edge of doubt in her voice that was immediately dispelled by her next words, 'Yes, you must be. Ramon said you were living here—'

'What is it you want?' Paula broke in tersely, marvelling at the cold dignity she was able to assume, and also wondering what was keeping her from saying she was Ramon's wife. 'As you know, Senor Calzada isn't in.'

'I'd like a drink.' Without ceremony, and taking Paula completely by surprise, she brushed past her and swept confidently into the lovely Blue and Gold Saloon. Barbs of jealousy seared Paula's nerves at the thought that this girl was so familiar with Ramon's house, the house in which she, Paula, was now mistress. 'When did your employer leave?' demanded Rosa, turning as she reached the centre of the room, 'and when will he be back?' Gliding over to a chair, she took possession of it, tossing away an unwanted cushion that missed the couch to which it was directed and landed on the floor not far from where Paula was standing. She looked at it, then walked away towards a cabinet containing drinks.

'You've been . . . seeing him?' She had no idea how a question like that escaped her and once it did she frowned, wishing she could draw it back.

'Of course,' with a disdainful flick of her dark eyes as she delved into her handbag for the gold case from which she extracted a cigarette. 'We're engaged to be married.'

Paula's eyes flew open, as well they might. She knew an almost hysterical desire to burst out laughing, and yet a great uneasiness was enveloping her, and she had a trembling feeling in the pit of her stomach, because she was recalling with vivid clarity her little access of suspicion that there was something about her marriage which she did not understand.

'Engaged?' she echoed at last. 'Since when have you been engaged to my—er—employer?'

Rosa was regarding her arrogantly through the film of blue smoke issuing from her lips.

'What's it to you?' she countered. 'Like Adela, you forget your place! It's always been the trouble with Ramon's secretaries—they've failed to keep in mind that they're only servants!'

Paula's teeth clamped together; this was obviously the moment to crush this girl's arrogance by revealing who she was, yet a mixture of curiosity and perversity made her say instead, 'It surprises me that although you look upon me as a servant, you're not averse to carrying on a conversation with me. Surely,' she added with a sort of acid sweetness, 'your dignity is suffering very greatly?'

Rosa's eyes narrowed to slits.

'You're impertinent!' she snapped. 'I shall certainly have something to say to Ramon about your conduct!'

Paula made no response, for although outwardly calm there was turbulence within her, as there was so much she did not understand. Also, this encounter with one of her husband's ex-girlfriends was something she had not contemplated and she was now wondering how many more would be calling here before it became known that Ramon was married. She reflected, too, on what Denis would say were he to learn that she had married a man—a foreigner—whom she knew to be a rake, a womaniser whose opinion of her sex in general was by no means flattering. She was even asking herself if she had done the right thing, aware that she had been carried away in that magic moment when Ramon had asked her to marry him. All her love had flowed through her veins when, after her few feeble hesitancies had been vanquished, it was released from the tight rein she had been keeping on it.

Attempting to hide her anxiety, she looked at the other girl, and after a moment heard her say, 'If Ramon takes my advice, he'll get rid of you right away.'

Paula said, watching the girl closely, 'That would be difficult because, you see, we signed a contract—'

'Contracts of that nature aren't worth the paper they are written on!' broke in Rosa impatiently. 'I might as well warn you that once Ramon and I are married you'll be sent packing, along with that insolent housekeeper of his!'

Paula was about to enlighten the girl but still she hesitated, and after a thoughtful pause she said curiously, 'You say you're engaged to my—to Ramon. I was not aware that he had been seriously keeping company with anyone.'

The girl stared straight at her.

'It so happens that Ramon and I were engaged some years ago—' She stopped abruptly, a gleam of anger in her eyes. 'You called him Ramon. He is Senor Calzada to you, girl! Just you remember that!'

Fury brought swift colour into Paula's cheeks. But it was the girl's first words that were making the most impression on her mind.

'Then you must be the girl who jilted him? You're married to someone else—'

'I *was* married,' corrected Rosa, cutting rudely into Paula's words. 'I'm divorced and, therefore, free to marry Ramon.' She frowned suddenly. 'How do you know about Ramon and me—and the broken engagement?'

'He told me about it!'

'I don't believe you. Ramon was never that personal with his secretaries. It must be the servants who've been gossiping to you!'

'You haven't said what you would like to drink,' Paula reminded her, still amazed by her own attitude of composure. 'I ask because I feel you are going to need something to sustain you in a moment or two.'

Rosa, about to extinguish her cigarette in the crystal ashtray which Paula had placed on the table at her elbow, sent her a startled glance.

'What are you talking about?' she demanded, raking Paula with her eyes. 'There's something strange about you.'

Paula nodded and asked again what she was drinking.

'Whisky—with a little water.'

Paula got it for her, placing it on a table at Rosa's elbow. She stood a moment as the Spanish girl picked up the glass and stared into its contents.

'You said just now that there is something strange about me.' Paula was walking away as she spoke. 'It's understandable that you should think so.' She reached a chair and sat down, crossing her slender legs over one another as she leant back against the cushions. 'You also said that you are engaged to Ramon—' She stopped to look straight at her, staring her out, determined to force her to lower her eyes, which she eventually did. 'That wasn't true—'

'Perhaps I should have said we are almost engaged,' amended Rosa, some of her self-confidence deserting her. 'I don't understand how you come to know so much about me—us—Ramon and I, but—'

'The reason,' broke in Paula quietly, 'is simple. Ramon and I were married recently, and naturally we had already exchanged confidences.'

'You—!' Rosa's face changed colour, a greyish tinge creeping into the glowing peach-tan of her cheeks. 'What did you say?'

'I believe you heard. Ramon is my husband.'

'I don't believe you!' cried Rosa in a rising voice. 'What kind of a joke is this? You must be out of your mind to make a statement like that!' Her eyes went automatically to Paula's left hand and she flinched.

'I assure you my mind is exceedingly clear on the particular matter of our wedding. You see, it took place less than a fortnight ago.'

Rosa's face was a ghastly yellow now, and her mouth was twisting convulsively.

'It—it isn't true. . . .' Every vestige of arrogance had dissolved; Rosa looked shattered, broken and ready to cry. But, glancing at Paula, sitting there so composed, she seemed to rally as swiftly as if a magic wand had been waved over her. She leant forward to stub out her cigarette; the somewhat fumbling action and the subsequent flexing of her white hands were the only sign of emotion she betrayed. But Paula had no difficulty in guessing at the severe turbulence that raged within her. For some reason—which Paula was hoping to discover—Rosa had believed that she was to have a second chance with the man she had jilted years ago, and there was no doubt at all that the information she had just received was a blow that had a nerve-shattering effect on her. 'I can't believe it's true,' she continued when she had taken a drink of her whisky. 'We've been going out together. . . .' Her voice trailed and she shook her head in bewilderment.

'Not regularly,' inserted Paula, thinking of the other women whom Ramon had been seeing since she came to work for him. There had been at least three.

'But he was serious,' stated Rosa vehemently. 'He said, only three weeks ago, that he loved me, that he had never loved another woman and never could.'

It was Paula's turn to change colour, the blood drained from her face. Like one lightning flash after another small incidents leapt into her mind, all combining to strengthen the possibility that this girl was speaking the truth when she maintained that Ramon had said he could never love another woman.

'My husband certainly loves me,' she had to say, desperately trying to convince herself rather than the other girl.

'No, you are quite wrong,' argued Rosa convincingly. 'Ramon never married simply because he loved *me*. When I was free we met again and he said he still loved me. We went about together and I suspected he was attempting to fight the attraction I had for him. But he could never succeed; his love for me was far too strong.' Rosa's voice had sunk almost to a whisper and it was plain that she was talking to herself, having forgotten Paula's presence altogether. 'But he did say, more than once, that revenge was one of the sweetest things in life. He said, too, that he was not the man ever to forgive a wrong done to him.' Rosa was staring in front of her with unseeing eyes. Fascinated, Paula watched her, avid for more even while her spirits were sinking with every word the girl uttered. 'He did it for revenge; he led me on by his charming manner, making me believe that he would not be able to resist me, that he must eventually ask me to marry him.' The vacant expression disappeared for an instant as she glanced across at Paula. 'Yes,' she murmured, becoming distant again, 'he did it for revenge . . . it's proved by the speed. He wanted to hurt me, and at the same time I am sure he was afraid . . . afraid that if he didn't marry quickly he would weaken. . . .' Rosa expelled a breath in a quivering sigh that was almost a sob. 'What a fool he is! Already he must be regretting it!' The voice rose louder, its sudden harshness a rasp on Paula's sensitive ears. 'Revenge, girl! If he's a fool, then you're a bigger one! Did you really believe he could fall in love with you in that short time? Or perhaps you didn't care. After all, his wealth would compensate, wouldn't it? Being Ramon's wife must be much more comfortable than being his secretary.' She spoke more loudly than ever, spitting out her words. Paula shuddered at her increasing lack of control as she flung herself out of the chair and began pacing the floor. 'He did it for revenge!' she cried, repeating it over and over again. 'Do you hear me—and understand? Are you coming from your fool's paradise and accepting what I say as the truth?'

'I do not accept it,' said Paula firmly, but she knew she lied. 'My husband does love me. He told me so.'

'He'd have to, wouldn't he?' The sneer in her voice was reflected in the dark Spanish eyes as Rosa added, stopping right in front of Paula's chair and standing over her, 'Only a stupid, gullible Englishwoman would be taken in like that. He's so handsome, isn't he? And English-women are highly romantic. Love is their very life, and you believed in a miracle—believed you'd succeeded where so many others had failed. Pompous creature! Why, you're little more than plain—the last woman who could attract Ramon.' The voice was frenzied now, grating on Paula's ears. She was trembling in every nerve in her body, sick with the feeling of emptiness in the pit of her stomach. For she was convinced, totally, that everything said by Rosa was true. Ramon *had* married for revenge, and Paula was the instrument of revenge. Without one thought for her feelings, or the hurt she would sustain, he had used her, callously, cruel-ly, to satisfy his insane desire to inflict hurt on the girl who had hurt him.

White to the lips, Paula flicked a hand to move the girl, who was so close she felt nauseated. Rosa stepped back and Paula rose from the chair.

'I'll ring for Adela to show you out,' she said

stiffly. 'There is nothing else for you and I to say to one another.'

'You're admitting that it's me he loves?'

'He loves me,' was Paula's quiet rejoinder as, walking across the room, she pulled the bell-rope.

'You might say it, but you don't believe it,' sneered Rosa. 'It isn't possible that he could love you because he loves *me*. Even Ramon can't love two women at once. He'll come back to me,' she added when Paula did not speak. 'He allowed his hate to override his love and decided to hurt me even though it meant hurting himself at the same time. He must be unhappy, and you must be able to see it—but perhaps you manage to turn a blind eye—' She broke off as the door opened and Adela, looking anything but happy, came into the room.

'Show this woman out,' said Paula, turning away so that she had her back to Rosa.

'Yes, certainly.' Adela looked at Rosa. 'This way,' she said abruptly.

'I don't need you to show me out,' she snapped, raking Adela's buxom figure contemptuously. 'I know my way around this house—all of it!'

Paula's teeth clamped together as fury rose within her. But her chief emotion was not anger; it was pain, deep and excruciating, and with it came quite naturally a sort of dull resignation that her marriage was already on the rocks.

'Please go,' she said, swinging around as she realised that Rosa had not moved. It was a moment alive with tension as the three women stood there: Adela looking as if she would like to throw the girl out bodily, Paula, her face devoid

of colour, willing the girl to leave before the
cloud of tears behind her eyes could break, and
Rosa, looking cool and self-assured, her dark
eyes filled with a sort of pitying disdain.

'He'll come back to me—have no doubts about
that.' She paused, obviously expecting to hear
Paula say something; when the silence continued she added, 'You believe all I've said, so what
do you intend to do about it?'

'Nothing,' returned Paula tightly. 'I am married to Ramon and it stays that way.' Her eyes
slid to the housekeeper's figure by the door. 'I
have asked you to go,' she reminded Rosa. 'If you
don't, I shall have to order you off the premises.'

'You're doing nothing?' Rosa's voice was a
snarl as her confidence turned to fury. 'You
intend to hold on to him—to a man who loves
another woman? I can assure you that he'll
already be regretting his impulsive action.' Her
dark eyes were pools of venom but Paula could
not see very well; her vision was impaired by the
mist of tears escaping from the cloud behind her
eyes. 'You'd play the dog-in-the-manger?' Rosa
went on, flicking an arrogant hand at Adela who
was trying to edge her from the room. 'Have you
no pride?' Paula merely turned away and walked
over to the window, her back to the room. She
was trembling from head to foot, mortified and
humiliated by the girl's outspokenness in front
of the housekeeper. 'Ramon will compensate
you financially, so you'll have much to gain.'

Money . . . Paula's lower lip quivered and she
sobbed on an indrawn breath. What could
money do to assuage the web of anguish surrounding her heart? Her tears came slowly and,
fiercely angry at her weakness at this particular

time, she swept them away, then turned again. Rosa came into her vision as the moisture cleared from her eyes; she seemed like a monster, some vile untouchable creature that ought to be crawling in the dark places of the earth.

Closing her eyes tightly, Paula shut out the fanciful vision and, with her head held high, walked across the room to where Adela was standing at the door looking extremely uncomfortable. Rosa was picking up her cigarette case and lighter from the low table on which she had left them. Her handbag was on the chair, its flap open; she slipped the two gold objects within, closed the flap, then stood arrogantly looking at Paula.

Without even saying goodnight Paula went from the room, into the hall, and made for the stairs. But Rosa had a parting shot to deliver; she flung it at her as Paula began to mount the stairs.

'If Ramon decides he wants a divorce, then you can be sure he'll have one, no matter what you might think to the contrary. He'll make your life such a hell you'll be glad to give him what he wants!'

Chapter Seven

It was late in the evening when Ramon returned. Paula, standing on the terrace, saw the car arrive, sweeping in through the Spanish-style wrought-iron gates to slide to a standstill on the amber-lighted forecourt. She saw him get out, walk with the light easy strides of an athlete towards the front door where he became lost to her view. Her heart was pounding wildly; she felt she would have done anything in order to escape the coming meeting with the man who had treated her so ruthlessly. She tried to move but failed, and so she just stood there, pain searing her heart, tears filming her eyes. Vaguely she was conscious of the scent of frangipani blossoms drifting over the garden, of the enchantment of the sky intruding through the delicate tracery of tamarind leaves, purple with silver-tinted cirrus clouds floating away like lace from a bridal veil. Paula could not appreciate any of the beauty, for all that stirred her senses was the duplicity of her husband, and a burning desire for her own revenge.

She turned only when she heard his voice, calling her from the living room of the house. Her heart seemed to turn a somersault as she attempted to envisage the scene about to be enacted between her husband and herself. Right was on her side, but she was convinced she would emerge from the encounter defeated.

Ramon was at the door; he smiled on seeing her and asked what she had been doing. It was very noticeable that he made no move to take her in his arms and kiss her. Anger and pain fought within Paula, and in this moment she felt she hated him, that she could have done him a physical injury if it had been at all possible.

'I was out on the terrace,' she answered dully. 'Er—did everything go well for you?'

He frowned at her manner.

'Is something wrong?' He subjected her to a searching, critical glance. 'You're pale. Are you not feeling well?'

Paula shook her head, her senses already madly alive to his magnetism, the power he had over her emotions.

'There *is* something wrong,' he observed. 'What is it?'

She passed her tongue over lips that had gone dry. How was she to begin? She had tried to rehearse what she would say but words had eluded her. She suspected it was owing to a burning desire for her own revenge, the form of which would not take shape. She would have liked to say nothing, to treat him coldly, even going to the lengths of saying she did not love him, but that would merely provide temporary satisfaction, since it could only be a matter of days at most before Rosa got in touch with him, and he would discover that Paula had met her, then decided to say nothing about her visit. In fact, Rosa could easily phone him tomorrow, at his office.

Yet the more she dwelt on the idea, the more it appealed as a heaven-sent opportunity. Yes, it *would* afford her only a temporary satisfaction, but even that would be better than nothing.

'I don't know why you should think there's anything wrong,' she returned indifferently, touching crimson hibiscus flowers Adela had set in a silver bowl. She felt oddly elated, and knew the cause was the doubtful pleasure of paying Ramon back for what he had done to her.

He glanced sharply at her, eyes narrowing.

'You've changed,' he stated. 'I demand to know what has happened while I've been away.'

She averted her eyes, admitting that it was natural that he should question her like this, when her whole manner towards him had changed. Before he went away she was the loving wife, pliably uninhibited; now she was aloof, smoothly impersonal.

'Nothing happened,' she replied off-handedly. 'I expect I'm rather tired.' She looked at him through her lashes. 'Can I have a drink, Ramon?'

'Of course.' Striding over to the cabinet, he poured her a drink, then one for himself. 'There must be something wrong,' he said on handing it to her. He was close, towering above her, an almost merciless quality in the intenseness of his dark, foreign eyes. Paula's heart jerked, but on the surface she was equally as calm as he.

'What is this all about?' She frowned at him

before taking a drink. 'You're acting very strangely, Ramon.'

His mouth tightened; there was a cutting edge to his voice as he said, 'It's *you* who is acting strangely. What's got into you?'

She made a little exclamation of asperity.

'Really,' she snapped, 'this is ridiculous! I've said there's nothing wrong. Why must you persist in saying there is?'

Silence, long and tense. Paula sipped her drink, blandly feigning ignorance of anything unusual in the atmosphere.

'You don't consider you owe me an explanation?' Ramon's voice was harsh but controlled. Lifting his glass to his lips he regarded her darkly over the rim of it.

She sent him a blank, bewildered glance.

'An explanation for what, Ramon? You seem to be making a mountain out of a molehill.'

She heard him give a little exclamation of anger, saw his lean brown fingers tighten on the stem of his glass and, glancing up, she noticed a nerve working convulsively in his throat. Deliberately she stood up, walked to the open window and stood looking out through the protective insect netting which formed a screen over it. In the garden lights flickered from among the branches of the trees. Moonlight reflected from the window of another room splayed a distorted oblong of silver onto a path carpeted with the misty blue-mauve petals of a jacaranda tree. It was sheer magic out there, a setting for lovers, a place to loiter for kissing and caressing and the exchange of whispered endearments.

Tears stung her eyes and she found herself

battling against the impulse to turn and run to him, to fling her arms around his neck and beg him to assure her in words of love that it was all a mistake, all lies she had heard. . . .

Just a dream that could never come true. Vividly she recalled her doubts now, doubts so slender they had eluded her efforts to gather them into more tangible form. There had been his brooding manner, that faraway look in his eyes; there was the lack of demonstrative gestures—the real endearments had been very few and far between. The abundance of her own love had carried her; she had been intoxicated to the point where Ramon's passionate lovemaking had blinded her to all else.

'Paula. . . .' His voice recalled her but she did not turn, for her eyes were misty with unshed tears, and her mouth trembled uncontrollably. How little she knew, when she had answered the advertisement, that she would find herself in such misery as a result of it. Her whole life was affected; she knew she would never be quite the same again, no matter what the healing years might do for her. And it did not help to know it was her own fault. She had plunged headlong into marriage with a man she scarcely knew, impulsively allowing her love to obliterate commonsense and caution. In effect, she had deliberately gambled with fate and with luck, and both had let her down.

Her heart skipped a beat as her husband came behind her, sliding his hands beneath her arms to fold themselves over her breasts. The male smell that hung about him stung her nostrils as the warmth of his hands burned through the

fine material of her dress. She tried to force
herself to twist angrily out of his arms, but she
quivered to his touch instead, conscious of him
with every quivering nerve-cell in her body. Yet
by sheer determination she was able to remain
stiff and unresponsive, aware that he must be
wondering why his touch was failing to affect
her, to ignite an ardent response which would
impel her to turn and cling to him, lifting her
face in eagerness for his kiss. Well, this at least
was some small degree of satisfaction to her,
knowing of his bewilderment as she continued
to remain coolly devoid of emotion while his
hands were temptingly caressing her breasts,
his fingers tight on the nipples. Up till now he
had believed that every woman he favoured
with his attentions would be thrown into ecstasy
by the caress of his hands, the closeness of his
body and its persuasive rhythmic movements.

'Something *is* wrong!' he said forcefully at
last. 'Just what is it, Paula?' He spoke in Spanish, his voice vibrant with anger. There was no
response from Paula—except that her body stiff-
ened more rigidly against his. 'Turn around!' he
commanded sharply, but he gave her no time to
obey as, gripping her arm, he jerked her body so
that she was facing him. She assumed a frowning countenance as she stared up into a face as
cold as tempered steel.

'Don't do that,' she cried. 'You're hurting my
arm!'

His teeth gritted together. Undoubtedly no
woman had ever treated him like this before.
Triumphant, Paula twisted her lips to produce a
mocking sneer, then instantly regretted her

impulse as, gripping her other shoulder, he
shook her brutally, his face a thundercloud, his
dark eyes pools of wrath.

'And now will you tell me what is wrong?' he
demanded, still gripping her shoulder as he
towered above her, a terrifying figure. Trembling violently from the punishment she had
received, Paula swayed against him, putting out
her hands to touch his chest for support. Without
warning she was swept into a savage embrace,
her head jerked backwards as he took a handful
of her hair and cruelly tugged at it. His head was
lowered; she twisted her face to escape his
lips, then gave a cry of pain and protest as her
hair pulled against her scalp. He took her lips
in savage, primitive domination, pressed his
body against hers, determinedly compelling an
awareness of the whip-cord strength of his muscles. She was swept into a tidal wave of passion
and desire which affected every cell, every
nerve in her body. But with a supreme effort she
managed to remain inert, determined to punish
him, to grind his pride into the dust. He continued persuasions that were by no means gentle,
ravaging her mouth, tormenting her body, bruis-
ing her with his tremendous strength, but Paula
still managed to resist. At last he held her from
him, his eyes dark with latent passion, his
breathing erratic.

'If you don't tell me what's wrong, I'll beat
you,' he threatened ominously at last, and he
gave her a little shake to add meaning to his
statement. Paula trembled, but she felt she
would even endure physical punishment if she
could hurt him as well. She was determined to
injure his pride in a way that would remain with

him forever, that would pay him for the pain and disillusionment she herself was suffering. The fact that it was all her own fault, that it would never have happened if she had relied on her intellect instead of her emotions, made no difference; certainly it did not lessen the enormity of the offence which Ramon had committed. And now, as she stared up into his face, noticing the tightening of the muscles round his mouth, the incised lines of harshness there which seemed to be accentuated by the taut set jaw and the granite-hard gaze, she knew her desire for revenge was equally as fierce and ruthless as any he had felt against the girl who had jilted him. And she looked at him with a sort of chill indifference as the lie left her lips.

'I had better tell you then, Ramon. The fact is, I'm regretting the impulse that led me to agree to marry you. I don't love you, and never did love you. I—I just thought it would be nice to think I had succeeded where all those others had failed.' She felt the pressure on her arms relax, saw the expression of bewilderment and disbelief slowly gather in his eyes. But her satisfaction was greatly reduced by the way she felt. She was trembling inside, her stomach rioting so that she felt almost physically sick; her legs were jelly, threatening to withdraw their support. What was he thinking, regarding her with an expression that had become inscrutable? When eventually he spoke, his voice was totally devoid of emotion.

'You expect me to believe you, Paula?' His hands slipped from her shoulders and she rubbed them, seeing in imagination the ugly bruises he must surely have inflicted.

'You've no alternative,' she answered carelessly. 'It's the truth—'

'It is not the truth,' he broke in, his fixed gaze
all-examining and she wondered if he saw deep
pain in her eyes, reflecting what was in her
heart. 'I know how a woman in love acts.'

'A great number of women have been in love
with you, I suppose, and so you believe you can
say a thing like that with confidence. But not
all women are alike. Englishwomen, for in-
stance—you have no experience with them.
We're very adept at the art of duplicity—'

'Stop it!' he thundered and she stepped away
from him, her heart racing even more madly
than before because she had never seen her
husband in this kind of mood and it terrified her.
He looked dark and almost evil with the shadows cast by the concealed lights washing the
deep, foreign-sculptured lines of his face in
sepia dimness. She shivered and her eyes were
troubled, but he remained unmoved by any
mental torment that was revealed to him by her
expression. *He has no heart,* she thought, *no
compassion—not even a pang of regret for the
way he had used her.* 'You're acting a part,' he
accused menacingly. 'I want the truth—or else!'

What was she to do? Her revenge—which
could be only short-lived anyway, for it was
certain that Rosa would contact him soon and
he would then guess why his wife had adopted
this attitude—seemed to be too difficult to
achieve, simply because Ramon refused to be
convinced. He was so sure she loved him, hence
his assertion that she was acting a part. If only
she could think of a way to force him to accept

that she did not love him, then victory would be hers.

'If you can give me one good reason why I should want to act a part,' she said at last, 'then I'd be very interested.' Moving over to where she had left her drink, she took up the glass, but made no attempt to sip the Martini it contained. The ice tinkled, the only sound other than the shrilling of cicadas in the trees outside the window.

'Something happened while I was away. . . .' Ramon's temper was under control now, and he was murmuring thoughtfully to himself. 'What could it be?'

She looked at him across the space dividing them. He was so attractive, now that he had moved from the shadows, and her heart and mind and emotions were difficult to deny. She wanted him so badly. To have his arms about her, his lips moist and tender on her mouth, his virile body taking possession of hers. . . . But that would mean nothing anymore. No, nothing, and if she were practical she would accept that the most sensible course would be to leave him, tonight, after a brief explanation, and return to her own country, for there was nothing left of her marriage but ashes, the burned-out remnants of romance.

Her lips tightened; she would not leave him yet! No, not until she had at least had some satisfaction, some modicum of revenge however slight.

'Something did happen while you were away,' she confessed, avoiding his direct stare. 'I discovered that I could not accept your—er—at-

tentions anymore. It's immoral without love—
Oh, I know that you have never considered it so,'
she added swiftly, 'but men are different, especially a man like you who has never been any
good anyway—' She broke off abruptly, catching
her breath as if the action could take back words
which could only ignite his fury again. Strangely, it did nothing of the kind. He remained cool,
aloof, but yet puzzled, and with a look of determination on his face that made her suspect he
might carry out his threat to beat her; that he
was capable of doing so she did not for one
moment doubt—and she also suspected that he
could continue inflicting the punishment until
she had satisfied his demand for an explanation.

'So you're not intending to accept my attentions anymore?' Soft the tone, but dangerous.
Paula did begin to wonder why she was continuing to hold out against him. 'Well, we shall see
about that a little later,' he added significantly
and with a twisted smile of arrogance. 'As your
husband I shall take what I want, and whenever
I like.'

The colour flooded her face at his way of
speaking. She turned from the dry humour of
his expression and sat down, sipping her drink
and deciding, for the very first time in her life,
that she needed something stronger—much
stronger! Recalling that Rosa had asked for
whisky she said, trying to keep her voice steady,
'Will you pour me a whisky, Ramon, please?'

Surprise lifted his eyebrows, but almost instantly he was saying, with maddening perception, 'You feel you need it? Well, you aren't
getting it. You can have another Martini if you
want.'

She flashed him a glance. 'Thanks for nothing! I shall drink what I like!'

He shook his head. 'You will drink what I allow you to drink,' he stated implacably.

'Then you can keep your Martini!' She sprang up to pace the floor very much in the manner of Rosa only twenty-four hours earlier. Her steps were short, agitated, her fists tightly clenched and fixed to her sides. 'I want whisky!' she flared, fully aware that she was losing control and yet unable to do anything about it. 'What has it to do with you what I drink?'

'As your husband, a great deal,' he returned mildly. 'I'm not having my wife drinking whisky—'

'Only your mistresses, I suppose!' It was out before she could even think about it. She was striding across the room with her back to him and, taken unawares, she felt herself brutally gripped by the arm and swung around to look up into the burning suffusion of colour that stained her husband's face. He shook her savagely until tears began to roll unchecked down her cheeks. And when at last he ceased, he had to steady her or she would have collapsed at his feet. She clung to the lapels of his linen jacket, crushing the material between frenzied fingers.

'I hate you,' she seethed, feeling as if every drop of blood in her body had surged to her heart, while her mind was enveloped in a searing vapour of fury that would have found an outlet in physical attack if she had thought there would be any chance of success. 'You're a beast—a vicious animal, and a cowardly one to attack someone weaker than yourself! Oh, God, why did I marry you?'

He released her and she noticed the strange and unfathomable twitching of a muscle in his throat. He turned, moving towards the open window as if wanting air. Silence reigned in the room, with tension high, sending off sparks, like electricity.

'It would appear,' said Ramon over his shoulder, 'that what really happened while I was away was that you had time to think, to form your own pictures of my past, and to decide that—*although you love me*—you've made a mistake in marrying me. You're afraid I shall be unfaithful to you. . . .' His voice trailed and it was natural that Paula should suspect him of secretly confessing that this could happen. But her main trend of thought was that he had unwittingly made things easy for her by forming his own conclusions regarding the dramatic change in her attitude towards him. 'Perhaps you're not entirely to blame for your fears—I have been a rake in the past. But you ought to have thought of it before you consented to marry me,' he added after a pause. 'Now that we *are* married, you will abide by your decision. I'm your husband, and in my country a husband has rights which his wife observes.' He turned then, and his dark eyes swept over her figure possessively, his gaze becoming fixed eventually on the tender curve of her breasts. 'Do I make myself clear, Paula?'

Her chin lifted.

'I hoped I had made *myself* clear,' she said tersely. 'I'm no longer willing to be your wife—at least, not in that way. It was impulsive of me to marry you, I admit, and it's true what you say about my fearing you will one day be unfaithful, because of your past. . . .' Her voice trailed, faltering to silence as she regretted the lies she was having to tell. It had all been so different; she had felt sure that he would always be faithful to her. If there had been any doubt in her mind to the contrary she would never have married him, no matter how strong her love for him might be. It would have been folly even more regrettable than the one she did commit.

'I think,' decided Ramon when she failed to continue with what she had been saying, 'that we will close the subject.' He glanced at the clock. 'Dinner will be ready in half an hour. We just have time to change.'

It was a silent meal, with Paula dreading what was to come afterwards. How could she fight a man as determined as this dark foreigner she had married? It was impossible, she told herself, looking at him across the table. He was her master and would remain so while she stayed here as his wife.

And yet, she was unable to resist fighting him when, in their bedroom, he took her possessively into his arms and, forcing her head back, tried to kiss her. Taking him by surprise, she was out of his hold and fleeing towards the door, scarcely knowing what she would do or where she would go, but instinctively making an effort to escape. With a muttered oath he was following her, his supple body carried with the agility of a jungle cat. She uttered a little scream even before he touched her and he stopped momentarily, his lower lip caught between his teeth. Then he reached out and took hold of her wrist, and she felt afterwards that he might have been gentle with her if only she had accepted his mastery, and the fact that he had a right to expect reciprocation from his bride.

But instinct once again came to the fore, urging her to struggle.

'Stop it!' he ordered, sharply. 'Do you want me to shake you again?'

'I expect you will do just that if the urge takes you,' she retorted, wondering vaguely where her courage was coming from. 'Coward that you are!' she added, twisting about with the instinctive, primitive compulsion of a wild female creature endeavoring to escape the inevitable.

'By God, Paula, you're asking for it! What are you trying to do—make me murder you!' Without affording her an opportunity of answering he jerked her protesting body against his, crushing it savagely until she uttered a little pleading cry as every bone affected seemed to be reduced to pulp. The blood pounded in her temples when her head was jerked so sharply that it seemed the muscles in her neck would snap.

'Leave m-me alone,' she whimpered, too weak and despairing to speak in anything but a low and husky tone. 'I—' The rest was smothered as his sensuous lips crushed hers in a hard, possessive kiss. She felt the lubrication of his mouth, forcing hers open, the contact of his teeth with hers before the roughness of his tongue sent a reluctant shudder of pleasure rippling through the entire length of her body. Still feebly trying to resist, she thrust her hands against his chest but they were caught and, without the slightest effort on his part, Ramon held them behind her back and looked down into her face with an expression of triumph that brought fury to her eyes. He intended to take her, and not gently as he had before, but with the arrogant domination of the conqueror whose intention it was to force total submission, to prove to her once and for all that he was her master.

'What are you going to do now?' he asked in some amusement as with the other hand he began to unbutton the front of her dress. 'Shall you still struggle to the end—or are you ready to admit that you would be wasting your energies?'

'I hate you,' was all she answered, in a voice that broke in the middle. 'I wish I'd never met you!'

He merely shrugged, more interested in what he was doing than in words. The dress she was wearing was long, nipped in at the waist and he appeared to be puzzled as to how to get it off. But just as she surmised, he soon discovered the zipper at the side and slid it down. He had to release her hands in order to slip the dress from her shoulders but she made no further move to struggle; she was overcome with weakness, and in any case, her emotions were already heightened by the contact of his hands with her flesh. She glanced down as the lovely dress dropped to the floor, obeying without protest when ordered to step out of it. She watched him flip it to one side with the toe of his highly-polished shoe and even that action seemed to accentuate the mastery he was so arrogantly adopting towards her.

'So you've decided that it's futile for you to fight me, eh?' His hands were smooth and warm on her arms, his deep-set foreign eyes almost lustful in their roving examination of her body. With a slick movement he had taken off her bra, and his lips twitched at the scantiness of the pretty piece of lace. She closed her eyes as he tossed it away, then quivered as his hand touched her breast, not moving, as if it were his intention to try her patience to the utmost. He knew so much about a woman's feelings! He could play with her for his own satisfaction and enjoyment until, crazy with longing, she would pander to his arrogant male ego by pleading with him to make love to her.

No, never that! He could do what he liked with her but she would never be reduced to submission as degrading as that.

His hands moved at last and it was Paula who felt triumphant now. She had managed to remain unmoving, as if she had no interest in what he was doing. He was exploring her soft body, his hands sweeping from her thighs, upwards to press into her waist, then to encircle her ribcage, his sensuous movements arrogantly possessive and masterful, his dark eyes all the time boring into her, watching her, alive to every change in her expression, every quiver of her soft young body. She had no illusions about his knowledge of her feelings; he knew he was awakening a desire for him that would crave fulfillment. He ordered her to put her arms around him and she obeyed, aware of his muscled strength beneath the evening shirt he wore. His mouth came down to possess hers and it seemed that every fibre was awakened when, at the same time, his hand slid down her back and she was brought even closer to his hard and sinewed frame. She was aware of the stirring rhythm of his movements, the erratic beat of his heart. His breath came more swiftly; his body pulsed with increasing ardour, infecting Paula's emotions and sending fire through her veins until she became lost in a sensuous, erotic longing for him.

'So you weren't intending to accept my attentions anymore?' His face was close to hers, amusement and arrogance mingling in his expression. 'How little you know yourself—wife!' With a swift and agile movement he had her in his arms, to stand for a long moment studying her with appraising eyes. 'Don't you feel rather foolish now?' he added, the gloating triumph in his tone abrasive on her ears. She turned away as he laid her down on the bed. He had proved his point, had brought her to surrender, but she would not afford him any more satisfaction than that, and so she made no answer, no sound at all until, a little later, a stifled moan escaped her, mingling with her husband's sudden gasp as their desire was fulfilled.

Chapter Eight

Paula awoke to the sunlight dancing on the wall of the bedroom, and to the perfume of flowers drifting in through the fly-screen covering the open window. Turning her head she looked at the tranquil figure of her husband and despite herself a great wave of love swept through her. The next moment, disgusted at her weakness, for the sensation was a weakness, she slid from the bed and went into the bathroom where she took a shower and was dressed before Ramon awoke.

'What time is it?' His eyes met hers through the mirror of the dressing-table where she was sitting, brushing her hair. 'Why didn't you wake me? There's a lot to do at the office today.'

'It isn't late.' She continued brushing her hair, avoiding his eyes now. 'I have about quarter to eight, but my watch isn't keeping very good time at present.'

'I'll buy you a new one,' he offered. 'There are some very excellent jewellers in San Juan as you probably know.'

She turned her head to look at him. So cool, leaning there on one elbow, watching her every movement! Last evening might never have taken place, much less the violent scene that had left her bruised and defeated.

'I don't want a new watch,' she said. 'I'll take this one in for repair.'

He shrugged and she turned away again, to pick up a perfume spray to use on her wrists and behind her ears. Her thoughts were in turmoil, because she felt she ought to leave here immediately, yet there was another side of her that could not bear the idea of leaving the way clear for Rosa to take her place. She thought of her attempts at revenge that had failed so miserably; she had intended repulsing her husband, hoping to succeed in convincing him that she did not want him. But she had been shown a very different side of his character, a frightening one which, although she knew him to be stern and forbidding at times, she would never have believed he possessed. He had taken what he wanted, gloatingly masterful as he proved, without much effort, that he could bring her to surrender just whenever he liked. A shuddering sigh escaped her; she shut out the scene and turned her thoughts to Rosa again. How long would it be before Ramon learned about her visit? Not long, she surmised, replacing the perfume spray and absently taking up the brush again.

'What are you thinking about, Paula?' Ramon's voice, cool and languid, came to her across the large, elegant bedroom.

'Why do you ask?' Paula went on brushing her

hair and for a space there was silence between them.

'Don't try my patience too much,' advised Ramon at last. 'You haven't seen the worst of me and that's a warning you'd be well-advised to keep in mind.' Rising from the bed, he unfolded his long length in cat-like movements and stretched luxuriously. His dressing-gown was on the end of the bed and he put it on, wrapping it round him and tying the girdle. Paula stood, watching him through the mirror, her body quivering suddenly and tiny beads of moisture coming on her upper lip. Why was she afraid like this? Ramon was perfectly calm, in full control of his passions and his temper, so what was the matter with her?

He came over, to stare at her in silence, his eyes expressionless, devoid either of warmth or emotion. Strange man! Unfathomable and distant, as if reaching out into the past. . . . It came almost as a shock to hear him say, 'You appear more beautiful every time I look at you.' His dark Spanish eyes roved; she was wearing linen slacks and a plain white shirt, and sandals that revealed peach-tipped toes. Her hair shone from the prolonged brushing she had given it; her cheeks were faintly flushed, the fine-textured skin flawlessly moulded to the classical bone structure of her face. She saw a muscle move unexpectedly in her husband's throat, was aware of his hand reaching out to draw her towards him, while with the other he relieved her of the hairbrush and laid it on the gleaming glass top of the dressing-table. 'But you seem afraid,' he added, as if suddenly noticing the moisture on her lip, the expression in her eyes.

'Fear does not become you. What is it?' Without awaiting an answer he was bending his head to take her quivering lips beneath his own in a long and passionate kiss that was yet gentle too, surprising her. She stared wordlessly up into his hard face when presently he held her from him; she felt small, defenceless, yet not now afraid of him. She saw the glimmer of a smile hovering on his lips and her response came hesitantly. If only he loved her! But he loved Rosa, of that Paula had no doubts whatsoever. He had married to spite her, to punish her for what she had done to him, but he loved her for all that.

He kissed her again, his arms tight around her, possessive and strong, his muscles tensed, and once again she was thinking that he had forgotten last night, and everything she had told him in her endeavor to get even. But he knew there was something wrong, and inevitably he would discover what it was—just as soon as his ex-fiancée telephoned him. He was kissing the delicate outline of Paula's breast and she quivered, caught in rapture that was pain.

'It'll be late when we get to the office,' she said, drawing away and becoming brisk. 'You've just said we have a lot to do.'

'Yes, we have.' He glanced at the clock and Paula wondered if he were estimating whether or not he would have time to make love to her. To her relief he said, 'I must shower and dress. I'll see you at breakfast.'

An hour and a half later Paula was sorting the mail when she came across an envelope that was addressed to her. She had written to several friends and this was one of the answers she had been expecting. Eagerly she slit the envelope and withdrew the single sheet of fine, airmail paper.

'Dear Paula,' she read. 'It was lovely to get your letter, with the colourful stamps and the foreign postmark. It caused quite a stir and the two boys were about to start a scrap as to which would have which stamp, so can you send the same two again and we'll have no further trouble. Well, you've certainly got yourself a lovely job, and your boss sounds like one of those unapproachables we ordinary girls can only stare at from afar and envy the girls who are attractive enough to win them for husbands. But of course, they are never faithful for long, as they have too many temptations. Their marriages break up and they try again and again. My Bill's a plain man, but nice and homey and I'm glad I've got him. How about you and Denis? Have you made any decisions yet? He wrote to my brother from some Caribbean island or other. Apparently his ship is on a Caribbean cruise so you could be having a surprise visit from him. I expect most ships call at Puerto Rico, as it sounds such a wonderful island with a great deal to offer. . . .' The letter went on to the end of the page, and over, and ended, 'The kids send their love along with Bill's and mine. Be happy! Love Janice.'

Paula held the paper in her hand, fleetingly scanning the words again. Handsome men like Ramon are never faithful for long. . . . Their marriages break up and they try again. . . .

Slowly she folded the letter and returned it to its envelope. What a fool she had been to marry Ramon! How was she to explain to her friends that she had been married and then separated in so short a time? She was positive it would be a short time, for Ramon must be regretting the impulse that had parted him from the girl he really loved. He would ask for a divorce, offering his rejected wife compensation by way of a financial settlement. It was the old, old story. . . .

The bell rang and she went to the inner office.

'I want you to go and choose a wristlet watch,' Ramon said, automatically glancing at the one she had on. 'Get exactly what you want and forget the price. All right?'

She began to shake her head, then suddenly felt stifled and the idea of getting out into the open for an hour or so appealed and she found herself saying, 'All right. I'll look, but I might not find what I want.' She had no intention of finding a watch to buy. Ramon could keep his presents for the woman he loved!

'I'm sorry not to come with you,' he went on, albeit rather absently as he fingered a pen lying on his desk, 'but I'm seeing a client as you know. Was there anything of importance in the mail?'

'I haven't really checked yet. I had one from a friend of mine.' A flicker of interest lightened his eyes. 'Male or female?'

'Female.'

'What about your friend Denis you spoke of? Hasn't he written?'

'No, but his ship's in the Caribbean; he might be seeing me, if the ship calls here, that is. Many ships do. There was one in yesterday; the town was crowded with the passengers. It must have been a very large ship—perhaps the Q.E.2.'

'Or maybe more than one ship was in.' Ramon

paused a moment, frowning. 'If this Denis does come to see you, you'll tell him it's all over, that you're now married and he mustn't try to see you again. Understand?'

Fury blazed at his words and the manner of their delivery. Who did he think he was dictating to! And he himself in love with another woman! Paula's first impulse was to tell Ramon she would see Denis just whenever she liked, and that, in any case, it was none of his business whom she had visiting her. But she refrained, wanting only to get away, and walk through the beautiful city of Old San Juan with its mellowed houses, its medieval atmosphere, and the citadel that rose above the city, dominating it. There was an abundance of flowers too, and the shops, a mingling of quaint and modern, were fascinating storehouses of treasures to take one's breath away.

She went out into the sunshine, and immediately the weight lifted from her. Once in the old city she sauntered along, not caring if she did not get back for hours. She had a very good excuse; she could not find exactly what she wanted, even though she had looked around all the jewellers' shops in the city. Telling the lie did not bother her in the least; she was too lethargic to worry her head about such things.

It soon became evident that a cruise ship had docked, for the passengers were in evidence in fair numbers, all staring about them or stopping to take snapshots. Paula wandered on, from one street to another, the sun on her face, the incomparable scent of frangipani in her nostrils. She felt thirsty as she passed a coffee shop and the delicious smell drifted out to her. She entered, and the first person she saw was Denis! She stood by the door and stared, watching the blue eyes widen with pleasure, the full mouth curve in a ready smile.

'Paula!' he exclaimed, rising. 'What a pleasant surprise! I had no idea I'd see you at this time. I intended phoning you at the office address you'd sent me, to see if it was possible for us to have lunch together, and then dinner tonight. We don't sail till one o'clock tomorrow morning—' He stopped to look her over admiringly. 'My, but this climate suits you! You've got a lovely tan.'

'So have you.' Suddenly she was happy, for here was someone to confide in. . . . How would he take her marriage? He had obviously not yet received the letter she had sent to Southampton, the port to which she had expected the ship to return after its voyage to the Canary Islands. 'I'm free for an hour or so,' she said, automatically glancing around. 'Shall we talk here or go somewhere else?'

He stared at her, seeming to be a trifle concerned by the look in her eyes.

'Is something wrong?' he asked anxiously.

She nodded.

'Yes, Denis, very wrong.' She glanced around again; the café was fairly full, with sounds of talk and laughter and music in the background. 'Let's find a quiet place,' she said. 'There's a very nice hotel just along this street; it's expensive and exclusive. We can talk there.'

He seemed to guess at her reluctance to talk as they went along, so he contained his curiosity until they were seated in the coffee lounge and had given their order. Very quiet music, and the occasional voice, were the only sounds to disturb them and Paula wasted no time in beginning to talk. Denis, his bronzed and rugged face set but his eyes narrowing and widening alternately as she progressed, sat there opposite to her, noticing that her eyes had become dull and deep in the pallid frame of her face. He seemed lost for words when at last she had finished her story. But eventually he spoke.

'So you're married. . . .' His eyes dropped to her left hand and his mouth muscles tightened. 'I—we . . . You and I, Paula, well, I know we weren't engaged, but—' He broke off, spreading his hands in a little helpless gesture. 'I felt, somehow, that we would eventually get down to the business of marriage.' He looked at her, his blue eyes moving from her face to her throat, and the delicate slope of her shoulders and then to her hand again, lying on the low table in a sort of listless fashion. Her wedding ring seemed to fascinate him but he made no comment, merely expelling a breath in what sounded like something between impatience and regret. His next words strengthened the impression. 'I should have done something positive, Paula. A girl wants to know where she stands. But for all that, I do feel you acted not only impulsively but irresponsibly.'

'There's no need to tell me that, Denis. Ramon's a rake and I knew it; I was told by Magdalena, the maid at the hacienda. And I had further evidence when women phoned him, and when he stayed out all night. On one occasion a girl slept in the hacienda, with him. Magdalena was sure of it.'

Denis was shaking his head in disgust.

'What on earth made you marry a man like that?' he said censoriously. 'It wasn't for money; you're not that kind of a girl.'

'No, it wasn't the money.' She paused a moment, feeling at first that she could not confide fully in her ex-boyfriend, and yet the reluctance soon passed, for they seemed closer now than they had ever been before. 'I fell madly in love with him—'

'Yes, you've already told me that,' he broke in roughly. 'But surely you could have seen the risk involved? You'd no need to commit the supreme folly of marrying him.'

'A woman in love doesn't see risks,' she began then stopped, having openly to admit that she did have a few misgivings.

'Then why the devil didn't you get away while the going was good?' he demanded. 'It was sheer madness to marry a rake!'

'I think he would have settled down with me if he'd married me for love,' she returned with a sigh. 'But it was this other business—the fact that he married me for revenge on the girl who had jilted him. How can he ever content himself with me when he's in love with someone else?'

'He hasn't given you any indication that he regrets the marriage?'

'No, but I'm sure he does. I believe Rosa when she says he loves her.'

Denis seemed a trifle perplexed as he said, 'It seems rather odd, when you think about it, that a man should rush into marriage with a girl he doesn't love, just to get even with a girl he does love.' He frowned and shook his bead. 'Not logical,' he ended briefly.

'What are you suggesting—that Ramon does love me? No, Denis, he doesn't. I can see that now, he isn't at all what the loving, tender bridegroom should be. . . .' Her voice trailed as the colour fused her cheeks, delicately. She was self-conscious over the words she had used, but Denis seemed not to have noticed anything untoward in her confession.

'From what you've said about this Ramon, he seems an odd sort of man. To harbour hate and bitterness for years and years—' He spread his hand disparagingly. 'It's proof of a very strange temperament. Surely you were aware of it?'

'I noticed nothing much at all,' she admitted self-deprecatingly. 'I was madly in love and even if I'd been warned over and over again I'd still have married him. I couldn't help myself.' She glanced up as the red-coated waiter appeared with the coffee on a tray. He put down the cups and saucers, the pots of coffee and milk, and the sugar-box. He straightened up, told Denis how much it was, and after receiving payment plus a tip, he smiled and went away.

Denis poured coffee for Paula and himself, his brow creased in a frown, and he spoke at last, after he had put sugar into his cup. 'You're still in love with him, obviously?'

'Yes,' she answered with a catch in her voice, 'I am.'

'So there's no hope for us, even when you get a divorce?'

'Divorce. . . .' Tears filmed her eyes. 'Married a fortnight and talking of divorce—it's terrible!'

'Ramon,' he said, unable to comment on that, 'surely he isn't thinking of a divorce yet?'

'No; in fact, he seems content as things are. But what will happen when Rosa phones him I can't say. It'll mean a showdown, of course, and he'll probably admit to being in love with her.'

'He's going to look darned foolish!'

'I've thought of that. But Ramon possesses an abundance of confidence that will enable him to overcome any embarrassment he might be feeling. I've never seen a man more self-possessed and sure of himself.'

'You've certainly got yourself into a mess,' he sighed, reaching for the coffee pot to fill his cup. 'I never thought, when I was so much looking forward to the ship docking here, in Puerto Rico, that I'd meet with information like this.' He looked directly at her, censure in his gaze. 'We'd been very good friends, Paula.'

'I agree, but as you've just said, a girl wants to know where she stands. I know we both felt that something serious would eventually result from our friendship, but neither of us ever mentioned marriage, did we?'

'No, but it was there at the back of our minds.'

'We weren't in love, Denis,' she said quietly.

'No, I suppose you must be right.' Again he stared directly at her. 'You never felt for me what you obviously felt for your—er—husband.'

'I was swept off my feet; I admit it. I knew I was falling in love with him and had in fact considered taking the prudent course and leaving him—that was when I felt there was no hope for me. All his other secretaries had fallen for him—'

'They had?' curiously and with a frown. 'You knew this?'

She nodded reluctantly.

'The woman who interviewed me in London told me, and warned me not to do the same.'

'For heaven's sake, Paula,' he exploded, 'wasn't that enough to put you on your guard!'

'Denis, it just doesn't happen that way. When *you* fall in love eventually you'll know what I mean.'

He merely let out an impatient breath and began drinking his coffee.

'The only thing I can suggest,' he commented after a while, 'is for you to throw up the job and return to England.'

Paula nodded in agreement.

'That's what I've been telling myself, but on the other hand, why should I leave the way clear for Rosa to take my place?'

'If what you say is true, then it's you who has taken her place.' Paula merely frowned and said nothing and Denis added, 'This girl was obviously led on by Ramon, who admitted he loved her, and so it was logical that she felt he'd ask her to marry him. It must have been a terrible shock for her to find that someone else had stepped in and become Ramon's wife.'

'She's not a nice person,' was Paula's defensive rejoinder. 'I'm very sure she'll never make Ramon happy. I told you she jilted him once, so how could she be really in love with him now?'

'Women are unpredictable. They don't seem able to make up their minds and stick to it.' *He sounds exasperated*, she thought, and supposed she could not blame him. This whole business must seem baffling to him, since he had a practical, clear-thinking sort of mind, and Paula had never known him go back on any decision he had made. He finished his coffee and looked at her inquiringly. 'Ready to go?' he asked and now his voice had an abrupt edge that sent her spirits into her feet.

'You—you mentioned our having lunch together. . . .'

'You've said you're supposed to be out looking for a watch; your husband'll be expecting you back.'

'There's no harm in him expecting. He'll not go without his lunch just because I'm not there.' There was a plea in her glance as she added, 'I'd like to have lunch with you, Denis.'

He hesitated, a sigh escaped him; she saw that he was feeling almost as unhappy as she.

'Paula,' he said, 'why couldn't you have waited? We were writing to one another—we promised we would, if you remember? I'm sure we'd have got down to the business of marriage once we'd satisfied our desires for adventure.' He stopped, expecting her to speak but she had nothing to say. The atmosphere between them was becoming warm and intimate; she felt closer to him than at any time before. She supposed she was trying to cling to something, like a dying man grasping at a straw; she had to keep afloat somehow.

'I believed we'd marry,' she had to admit. 'And when I first began working for Ramon all I could think of was the wonderful salary I was getting; it would be so easy to save, so that if you had wanted to marry me I'd have been able to contribute to the expenses. . . .' Her voice trailed on a little sob. 'Life was so uncomplicated before—before I began to be affected by Ramon's attractions.'

Reaching across the table, he took her hand in his.

'I want to kiss you,' he confessed. 'I want to see those lovely eyes happy again. Paula, one can forget, you know. It's been a rotten experience, but people have been surviving bad experiences since the world began. Leave him, dear, and let you and me start again. Get your divorce and we'll marry. I know we can make a go of it.'

So confident. Paula sighed but said nothing to deflate his optimism. They weren't in love and never had been, but they did have a great deal in common. Could they make a go of it, as Denis was predicting? Undoubtedly Denis had a lot to recommend him: he was sincere, reliable and staunch. She would never have to fear unfaithfulness.

'I'm still in love with Ramon,' she could not help reminding him, an unconscious note of apology in her voice.

'I know, dear, but you'll forget all about him in time. Look,' he said on sudden impulse, 'I'll make this my last trip. We'll both go home and take up where we left off. How does that appeal to you?' He looked earnestly at her and she caught her underlip between her teeth, trying to hold back the tears that threatened. *He was so good, too good for her*, she thought, wishing with all her heart she had never set eyes on Ramon.

'I don't know what to say,' she faltered. 'Is it really possible, Denis—to take up where we left off, I mean?' Her heart was lead, her mind unable to function properly, for although she could not bear to lose Denis, too, at the same time she felt that if she were to make any promises she might merely be selfishly using him, because of her present need, and that at some later date she would be forced to let him down, because she was still in love with Ramon and no one would ever take his place in her heart. Yet even while all this was passing through her mind her thoughts raced on and she was seeing a day when the pain would have healed and she was able objectively to look back without hurt, and so perhaps, one day, she and Denis might be able to take up where they had left off.

'I think it's possible,' he was saying, his fingers moving over the back of her hand. 'Come on, buck up,' he encouraged. 'Let me see that lovely smile of yours.'

She obliged and he seemed pleased.

'You're so good,' she murmured. 'I wish . . .'

'That we'd become engaged before we both started on all this?'

'In a way, yes. But as I've said, we weren't in love.'

'We weren't far off it. If we hadn't separated the way we did we'd have been in love by now.'

'Perhaps we would,' she returned, but was by no means convinced.

He became thoughtful for a moment or two.

'This feeling you have for Ramon could be infatuation,' he suggested at length. 'It's the sort of thing that's happening all the time. In fact, it happened to me once—when I was nineteen.' He looked rueful, falling into a mood of retrospection. 'She was smitten, too. We both laughed at it afterwards, and said a friendly goodbye.'

Paula regarded him with a new interest.

'You don't seem the kind to be infatuated,

Denis. You're always so sensible and practical, looking beyond the immediate present.'

'I admit I usually do like to be practical, to try and visualise the outcome of my actions. It's the only way to avoid disaster, but on the other hand, human nature being what it is, one can't always control one's impulses.'

'Like me,' she uttered with a break in her voice.

His face shadowed.

'It'll pass,' he said reassuringly after a pause. 'Come on, let's go and find a place for lunch.' He gave her hand a final squeeze before withdrawing his own; Paula felt its loss and knew for sure that she needed Denis at this crucial time in her life.

It was past three o'clock when she entered the office. Ramon was in his private office, with a client, but as soon as the man left Ramon told his wife to stop what she was doing and come to him. Her heart missed a beat at his tone of voice, which was grim to say the least.

And his expression matched it. A little of the colour left Paula's face as she closed the door of his office and turned to face him. Rosa had been in touch, obviously.

'Sit down,' he said darkly, 'I have a lot to say to you.'

She obeyed, facing him across the desk. Her heart was beating overrate, and she wondered if she looked as white as she felt. Yet a spurt of anger brought two spots of colour instantly to her cheeks as it became clear to her that if either of them should be feeling uncomfortable it should be her husband. He was the guilty one, and it was he who should offer explanations and apologies.

'You've heard from your old flame,' she said, breaking the silence.

The dark foreign eyes were narrowed, looking directly into hers, but she met them unflinchingly; she was quite ready to do battle with him.

'I have had a telephone call from Rosa Donado,' he answered softly. 'Why didn't you tell me she had called?'

'I chose not to.' As she expected, her brief rejoinder brought a glint to his eyes.

'Your reason being that you wanted to hit back at me. I knew you were playing a part, but I was completely baffled. It's all clear now that I've learned of Rosa's visit and discovered some of the things she said to you.'

'Shall we cut out the irrelevancies,' suggested Paula evenly, 'and get down to what's important? First, I would like to hear your admission that you lied when you said you loved me.'

Silence followed her words, lasting for several seconds before being broken by Ramon's finely-modulated voice saying, 'Rosa must have talked of more than she admitted on the phone—'

'You haven't answered my question,' interrupted Paula and his jaw muscles tightened.

'Be careful how you talk to me,' he warned in a dangerously soft voice which had no effect whatsoever on his wife.

'I'm the injured party, Ramon, and don't forget it! You might believe you can browbeat me by that arrogant, superior manner but I'm right. Admit that you married me for revenge, that it is Rosa you love—admit it!' She spoke forcefully, surprising herself even more than

him. She had risen to her feet and was looking
down at him, aware that he would hate that. If
anyone were to look down it should be he. 'Your
expression's enough,' she added with a glance of
contempt which, to her intense satisfaction,
brought a swift and deep wave of colour creeping into the deep tan of his face. 'If anyone
looked guilty, you certainly do! Aren't you
ashamed of yourself—using an innocent person
for your own vile ends?'

Ramon stood up, and she saw a nerve pulsating in his cheek, completely out of control.

'I admit it all,' he said, and a deep silence
dropped on the room. For Paula suddenly realised that until this moment of confession on her
husband's part, hope had remained alive, deep
in her subconscious, that it was all a mistake,
that Rosa had lied and that Ramon would refute
it all and she, Paula, would believe him. Yes, in
spite of all she had said to herself and to Denis,
in spite of the despair, the hopelessness and
acceptance of Rosa's information, there had
been a glimmer of hope within her, loitering
there, at the back of her mind.

Now all hope was dead. Ramon had admitted
that what Rosa said was true.

Paula turned away, despair and resignation
firmly taking hold, colouring her reactions and
she heard herself saying, 'Go back to her, then,
and I'll play a similar game. Denis is here, in
San Juan—I've been with him all morning and
we had lunch together. We'll have the rest of the
day together—he's phoning me in an hour's
time.' She swung around and looked at him
hostilely across the wide, highly-polished desk.
'Go on, get back to her! You told her only three

weeks ago that you loved her! You were thinking of marrying me at that time, weren't you? It's so easy to see now what the hurry was! You know your own wretched weakness, knew you might succumb and marry her! Well, you'll marry her in the end, but not as soon as you would wish. I shall fight the divorce! I'll make you wait just as long as the law will let me—get that!' Her voice was loud, quivering with the fury awakened in her. She scarcely knew what she was saying, but through the blazing conflagration of her anger there did emerge the fact that, no matter what she said she had no intention of delaying the divorce. She would get rid of him as quickly as she could.

'I have no wish to marry Rosa,' came Ramon's quietly-spoken response. 'I am not contemplating a divorce, Paula, so you can get the idea right out of your mind.'

She glared at him, hating his calm composure, and the way he stood there, in a magisterial attitude, just as if she were the culprit instead of he.

'You're merely saying that. You're in love with Rosa so obviously you want to marry her—'

'Had I wanted to marry her,' interposed Ramon smoothly, 'there was nothing to stop me. It should be plain to you that I had no intention of marrying her.'

'I've just said you were afraid of weakening. Of course you'd rather be married to her than me, it's only logical. But you wanted to be revenged, didn't you?'

'Yes, Paula, I did. I'm a man who finds it impossible to forgive an injury done to me. I believe I made that clear to you early in our

relationship. Yes, I always meant to be revenged
on Rosa if ever the opportunity arose. She played
right into my hands after her divorce. She got in
touch, believing that the only reason for my not
marrying was because I was still in love with
her—'

'Which was true!'

'Yes, it was true. But what was also true, and
what Rosa did not know, was that nothing—
nothing—would have induced me to marry her
after what she had done to me all those years
ago.' He stared at Paula, his mouth tight, his
jawline taut and hard. He looked so darkly
formidable that Paula shivered inwardly, and
wondered if she ought to practice caution and
not arouse emotions that might result in her
own discomfort. She already knew about his
temper, to her cost; it was something to be
avoided, certainly not deliberately aroused.

'But you did marry me to be revenged on her?'
Ramon nodded his head instantly.

'I have already admitted it.'

'How can you stand there and say these things
to me?' she cried, the anguish in her heart more
pronounced in her consciousness than the fury
that consumed her. 'You knew I—I . . .' Her
voice caught, then broke altogether.

Again he nodded, appearing to care nothing
for her sudden distress.

'Yes, I knew you loved me. But you must
remember that every secretary I have ever had
has fallen in love with me,' he went on contemptuously. 'I didn't give you the slightest encouragement, so if you fell in love with me it's
entirely your own fault. Didn't it ever occur to
you that I am not a man to fall in love?'

Paula shut her eyes tightly, the pain he had inflicted almost physical, the knot round her heart so tight it seemed the blood had stopped flowing. She swayed, wanting to sit down, but by some miracle she was able to conjure up a degree of strength so that her voice was amazingly steady, considering the pain that was catching her throat.

'You've always regarded me with contempt, then? I'm no different from the others?'

'I believe I have said you are very different from the majority of women I have met—'

'And had affairs with!' she could not resist flinging at him.

'Be careful, Paula,' he advised in a softly dangerous voice. 'Don't push me too far.'

'And don't you put on that superior attitude!' she returned fiercely, a burning vapour of fury suffusing her mind. 'I'm the injured party! I've been used, for your puerile desire for petty revenge!'

'Puerile?' The word inflamed him and he strode round to her side of the desk to tower above her. 'Don't you dare use a word like that to me again!'

'Aren't you puerile?' she ventured, her heart racing at the menacing closeness of him.

Losing control, he shook her, but she kicked out and had the satisfaction of seeing him flinch at the contact of her shoe with his shin. He let go of her and she swayed a little, grasping hold of the top of the desk to steady herself.

'I'm getting out of here,' she cried. 'I'll wait in my office for my phone call, and then I'm going out to meet Denis—'

'I think not,' interposed her husband smoulderingly. 'I warned you that you were finished with him, now that you're married.'

She stared at him in amazement.

'Surely you're not intending to adopt this dictatorial husband attitude,' she sneered. 'Any rights you had over me you have just forfeited by your admissions. We're nothing to one another anymore—we never were, were we? I was the fool, but I'm not a fool any longer! I shall do just as I please, and go out with a dozen men if I want!' Even as she spoke she stepped back strategically towards the door. 'If you so much as touch me,' she said on noting his expression, 'I shall scream so loudly that everyone in this office block will come running!'

That seemed to sober him; he returned to his side of the desk and regarded her across it, his dark eyes probing into hers.

'You say you've been with this Denis all the morning? I sent you out to choose a watch.'

'Keep your presents!' she flung at him. 'Give them to Rosa—or any of the other women you have in tow! Was the watch to be a conscience present?' she asked as the thought occurred to her. He made no answer and she flashed, 'You have no conscience, though! You're rotten through and through!'

'All right—' His hand was raised in a gesture of exasperation. 'You've had your say, aired your grievances. And now, let us get down to what's important, what affects us personally, you and me. I've already said I'm not intending to have a divorce; I have said also that you're different from any other woman I have known. You satisfy me in many ways, and I know I satisfy

you. We can live amicably—we did so until Rosa
came into the picture—'

'You must have known she would. You led her
on, and it was only to be expected that she
should come to you when you hadn't contacted
her. You must have known that she and I would
meet.'

An impatient frown crossed his face.

'Can we leave Rosa out of it? I've finished with
her and told her so this morning, on the telephone. I'm concerned only with you and me. We
can carry on as we did before I went to Haiti. We
were reasonably happy, you must agree with
me?' he added looking at her steadily.

'It was all a veneer on your part,' she returned
bitterly. 'Pretense, that's all. You said you loved
me, because you had to or I'd never have married you. And then, afterwards, you had to be
nice to me, hadn't you, in order to deceive me?
But I felt there was something wrong, because
although you were indulgent and affectionate I
was conscious of something missing in our—our
union. . . .' She faltered to a stop and her teeth
clenched together, an automatic action meant to
help bring her emotions under control. She was
very close to tears, because of the cool dispassionate way he was staring at her, the chill
isolation in which she felt herself to be poised.
She supposed the years would dissipate her
misery, but that was scant consolation to her at
this moment in time. 'It was an intangible
thing,' she continued presently, 'a nebulous link
th-that was m-missing . . . all the time. . . .' Her
voice trailed again, reflectively, and without any
awareness of the action she was pressing fingers
to her temples, because they were throbbing

suddenly with the tremendous effort she was
making to hold back the tears. Her eyes moved,
to meet his, her long curling lashes glistening,
and tipped with gold as a shaft of sunlight
filtered the foliage of trees outside the office
window. Spiky shadows fell on to her cheeks;
she saw her husband's eyes become fixed, noticed again a nerve pulsating in his cheek and
wondered at his thoughts. He did not hate her; of
that she was sure, but neither did he love her
and she knew that, emotionally, he would feel
nothing if she went away this moment and he
were never to set eyes on her again. Nevertheless, he was by no means indifferent to her.
Firstly, she satisfied him in many ways—he had
just said so, and one of those ways was that she
appealed to him physically, in a different manner from that of any other woman he had ever
known. Secondly, he was sorry for her. Yes,
there was pity in his eyes, although it was not
openly apparent. Anger rose; pity was the last
thing she wanted from him! Let him save it for
himself because she intended to make him
suffer if she could.

'I admit I acted a part,' said Ramon frankly.
'But for all that we were reasonably happy. You
have much to gain by marriage to me. You'll
never have to work again—I intend to get another secretary,' he added swiftly when she was
about to interrupt. 'I shall try a man; it might be
the answer. And as for us—well, we can get
along all right. After all, love doesn't last, and
although you're in love with me at present, it'll
soon pass, and then we shall settle down to a
pleasant sort of companionship, have a family,
and probably remain together all our lives—'

'Stop it!' cried Paula. 'That's no kind of marriage! And do you suppose I want children by a man who doesn't love me?'

'Many women have children by men who don't love them,' he returned casually. 'There's a great deal of pretence in most marriages, Paula. A couple marry believing they're in love; within a year at most the novelty's beginning to wear off, and after another few months they're wondering what they saw in one another.' He paused, a smile of sardonic amusement curving the fine outline of his mouth. 'It's happening all the time, all over the world. Many of these couples stay together, more because marriage becomes a habit—a way of life—than anything else. Habit is hard to break, remember, so they carry on, often going their separate ways but sleeping together. They raise a family, and often when the family is growing up there comes the sudden realisation that they—the parents—are losing their youth. They discuss separation, each picturing a fresh start with a new partner. But then they think of the children, and if they're responsible people, they decide to stay together until the children are off their hands. By that time they probably no longer want the break. The woman especially is afraid, because she's lost her bloom and feels she might be unable to attract another man. The husband has probably fallen into a pleasant routine of nights out with his friends, of golfing holidays—' Ramon spread his hands expressively. 'It isn't new, all this,' he said seriously. 'There's no sense in your being an idealist in a world where realism controls everything.' His voice had softened, she noticed, as if he were sorry for her, and her eyes moistened as they stared dumbly into his. She felt the presence in her heart of a great sadness, pressing down until the weight hurt with the intensity of physical pain. She wanted to weep for her own lost dreams. Ramon was so cold-blooded and practical about it all—about life and marriage . . . and love, which he genuinely believed could never last. His bitterness was so deep that nothing could penetrate it, no woman's love could vanquish it. It was with him forever; he had learned to live with it so that it was a part of him, inseparable from other emotions. She swallowed convulsively, conscious of his dark eyes fixed upon her. She tried to speak but could not trust her voice not to break and instead she found herself dwelling on her own ideas of love and marriage. When she found her man he would be her all, her life, and she would serve him until the end. She had married Ramon with hope in her heart, aware of his past but sure her love was strong enough to make him forget everything but the joy of her, the anticipation of a happy life with her by his side, sharing the sunny days, laughing at the rain. Yes, she was an idealist, and now she had been disillusioned because the man she had fallen in love with had no heart, no desires other than those of the flesh. He would always want a woman to mate with, yes, until he was old, but there was little else he would want from her.

But her thoughts went back to what he had been saying. It was true that they had much in common. He had been *reasonably* happy, while she in her blind innocence had been *deliriously* happy, this in spite of her faint misgivings and the fact that her husband could have been a little more loving and affectionate. She supposed, looking back now, that in her heart she had been optimistic, cherishing the hope that Ramon would eventually be the adoring husband of her dreams.

'What are you thinking, Paula?' Ramon's voice recalled her and her eyes lifted.

'We ought to separate,' she murmured, watching his reaction carefully.

His eyes chilled; his mouth compressed.

'I do not believe in divorce,' he said abruptly.

'I believed, when Rosa was telling me everything, that you would want to divorce me and marry her—' She broke off on hearing his exclamation of anger.

'Forget Rosa,' he commanded, and now his voice was imperious, dictatorial. 'She meant mischief, obviously, but I have so little interest that I don't even want to know what she did say. I gathered enough when I spoke to her on the phone this morning. She'll not trouble either of us again. I've had my revenge and it was sweet. . . .' His voice trailed on a strange little note and as she watched his expression Paula felt sure there was regret in his eyes. Regret? For hurting her the way he had? Perhaps there was some small degree of softness and compassion in him after all. And if there was . . . ? Could there be hope for their marriage?

Sadly she shook her head. Pity he might be able to portray, but love had become completely foreign to his nature. And pity was the last thing she would ever want from him.

'I'm going out to dinner with Denis this evening.' She spoke sharply, suddenly desiring only to hit back. If she could not touch any sensitive chord that would inflict pain, then at least she could attack his pride.

A silence followed; she felt the tension in the atmosphere before her husband broke it by saying, 'You're my wife, Paula, and you'll obey me. I forbid you to see this man again. When he phones I shall speak to him.' So quiet the tone but authoritative, matching the implacable look in his eyes. She moistened her lips, nerves leaping. For she was under no illusions about Ramon's innate sense of mastery where his wife was concerned. She was his possession and it would not take much for him to demonstrate the fact.

'I've promised,' she began. 'Besides, I don't owe you anything anymore.'

'We both owe each other loyalty,' he said, and her eyes darted to his in a look of astonishment.

'You can say that? You're speaking of a marriage based on nothing firmer than sand!'

'As far as I am concerned,' he said implacably, 'it's permanent, no matter what you believe to the contrary. Think about it—think well, remembering what I have said. You will never attain perfection so you might as well abandon the idea. Make your decision to stay with me and keep to it. You will benefit in the long run, and if you will use your logic, you'll very soon see the sense of what I'm saying.' He began to move restlessly, his eyes flicking to a document lying on his desk; he was obviously becoming impatient to get back to his work.

'I'm to settle for security? Is that what you're telling me?'

'That, and other things. Physically you're satisfied with me, just as I am with you—'

'Need you be so clinical about it?' she flashed, a wave of crimson staining her cheeks.

He smiled as he stared at her, a glimmer of amusement in his eyes.

'It's no wonder I find you different,' he said softly and with a little sigh of pleasure. 'I shall never regret marrying you.'

She stared at him in bewildered silence, her lovely eyes darkened by the cloud of tears pressing against the backs of them. She shook her head and murmured presently, 'I wish I could understand you, Ramon. . . .' Mechanically she got up to stand with her back to the filtering sunlight, her ears catching the lazy murmur of insects in the branches of the trees outside the open, netted window; there was a dazed expression on her face, entreaty in her wide-eyed stare, a certain element of helplessness and vulnerability in the pallor of her cheeks, the softly-parted lips. 'What kind of a man are you?'

He came towards her from his side of the desk, his mind no longer on his work.

'Perhaps you will understand me one day.' His voice had a different quality about it, his smile was neither amused nor sardonic. 'And perhaps if *I* had understood *you* I might not have used you. I might have found someone else. And yet, as I've just said, I don't regret marrying you.' His hand was extended, its open palm an invitation. Paula stared at it, her lips quivering. And then she found herself obeying the impulse of her heart and putting her hand into it. The contact sent feathery ripples along her spine, and when he drew her to him and tilted her chin she had no desire to resist him. His lips were moistly sensuous on hers, his hand in the small

of her back warm and intimate. The fingers of
his other hand found sensitive places on her
nape, then her ear and the tender curve of her
throat. She quivered against him, fully aware
that this tacticle stimulation was deliberate, a
complement to the subtle persuasion of his
words. There was no doubt about his wanting
her to stay with him, and, in spite of her deep
unhappiness, she could not but feel gratified
that she had a certain attraction for him, an
appeal which was an absolute safeguard against
the danger of any other woman usurping her.
Yet it was a scant consolation to a heart craving
for his love. . . .

His hand was on her throat, caressing it
lightly; his lips were leaving moisture on the
lobe of her ear. Before she realised it, her need of
him was overshadowing all else and doubts of
unhappiness were being pushed into the depths
of her consciousness. It was a temporary state,
but after all the time was *now*. She clung to him,
lifting her face for his lips to meet hers as she
strained her body to meld with the iron-hard
maleness of his long and slender frame. That he
held her captive sexually she could not deny,
and life without his caresses seemed in this
moment of longing to be little less empty than
life without his love.

'You'll stay with me, my wife.' Not a question
but a categorical statement voiced with supreme confidence. How sure of himself he was!
The perfect lover whose past experiences had
left him in no doubt whatsoever of his superiority over the opposite sex.

Paula did not argue with him; she was swayed
by the delicious ecstasy of his nearness, of his

arm about her, his mouth close to her temple—
the touch of a butterfly wing that felt like the
waft of his breath rather than the touch of his
lips. Paula's own breath came swiftly as she felt
his body pulse with ardour, and she strained
against him, yielding to the movements of his
hands as they slid down in sensual and masterful persuasion.

'I love you,' she whispered, but silently, and
her eyes filled with tears.

'Tell me you'll stay.' Ramon held her at arms'
length to look deeply into her eyes. She saw his
sudden frown and realised that he had noticed
the tears sparkling on her lashes.

'*You've* said I'll stay,' she reminded him.

He nodded in a rather absent way.

'But I want you to say it.'

'I'll stay . . . for a while.'

'For always. We shall start a family at once. It
is time I thought of an heir.'

'Have I no say in it?' she did not want to start a
family, because even though at this moment she
felt she could never leave her husband, there
lingered in her mind the undoubted fact that she
might not always feel like this.

'You will do what I want.' His voice and
manner had changed. Paula's heart grew cold as
she looked up into eyes devoid of feeling, and
heard his hard, objective tone as he added, 'A
man in my position should have a son to follow
him. The Hacienda Calzada has been in my
family for generations; it should remain so for
generations to come.' He was all arrogance, the
classical regularity of his features branding him
what he was: an aristocrat.

Paula could find nothing to say, and in any

case the phone was ringing in the outer office—
her office.

'I'll take it,' said Ramon decisively as she
began to move.

Her lips tightened.

'It'll probably be Denis,' she began.

'That is my reason for answering,' he said,
making for the door with long athletic strides
which covered the distance across the room in
seconds.

'Please, let me speak to him,' begged Paula.

Ignoring her request, Ramon picked up the
receiver.

'Let me speak to him,' pleaded Paula again.

'Yes, my wife is here, but she has nothing to
say to you.' Ramon's imperious voice was a rasp
on Paula's ears. She hated him for not listening
to her plea. 'I'm afraid not. Good afternoon.' As
the receiver clicked into place Paula experienced a fierce, uncontrollable urge to retaliate
and without one second's hesitation she lifted
her hand and struck him across the cheek.

The dark foreign eyes blazed, then fixed hers
in a piercing stare of disbelief. She expected a
shaking, but instead she was gripped painfully
by the wrist and jerked roughly against the
granite hardness of his chest, her breasts flat-
tened, her bones almost cracking under the
strain. Her head was jerked back when he
cupped her chin, and her mouth ravaged with
brutal and primitive uncontrol. Sheer rage drove
him and she was crying softly when at last he let
her go. She closed her eyes against the blazing
fury of his gaze, and the tears oozed from
between her lashes to roll one after the other
down her pallid cheeks. A sob escaped her, and

yet again she knew a wild and fierce desire to be revenged on him.

'I'm—going h-home,' she quavered, putting her face in her hands and weeping into them. 'Don't ask me to stay here—don't try to make me! I shall scream if you do. I've had as much as I can stand and I want to get away from you!'

'I'll take you home,' he offered, fury causing his voice to vibrate. 'Just let that be a lesson,' he warned, as if he had to. 'Never has a woman done a thing like that to me before—'

'Well, you did say I was different!' she reminded him with an unexpected spurt of courage. 'I shall do it again if I feel like it!'

'To your cost,' he gritted. 'I've warned you already that you haven't seen the worst of me.'

'I'm going home,' she said again, then added before he could speak, 'and alone. I couldn't bear your company for another minute!'

'You're in no fit state to go out alone,' he began when, taken unawares, he was pushed against her desk and she was at the office door, wrenching it open. The long lobby was ahead and she knew he would catch her. Wildly she glanced around, saw the ladies rest room and dodged into it. There was another door, leading to another corridor and she was through it in seconds. She never stopped until she had reached the street and when she turned her head Ramon was nowhere in sight. With a pounding heart and rioting pulse she found a seat beneath a tree and sat down, wondering if her nerves would ever be right again. It was too much; life could not go on like this, she decided. She would get away; it was the only logical thing to do.

It was an hour later, when she was strolling along a narrow street in the old city, that she caught sight of Denis, looking into the window of a souvenir shop. She stopped, scarcely able to believe her luck, and only now aware that, subconsciously, she had been looking for him.

'Denis!' She had run to him, afraid he would move and be lost to her sight in the press of people milling about. 'Oh, it's a—a relief to see you—' She stopped to get her breath back, aware of his surprise, his pleasure and his concern.

'Paula, dear, what happened? Your husband—he was obviously not allowing you to speak to me.'

She glanced around fearfully, as if expecting Ramon to appear at her side.

'Let's find somewhere quiet, and secluded,' she begged. 'Oh, Denis, it's been awful—you have no idea! She started to cry and felt the comfort of his arm about her shoulders.

'Don't cry, darling; we'll sort it all out when you've explained. I've been so troubled, not knowing how to get in contact with you, and this must be fate—our meeting like this. I'm taking you over to that car park. I hired a car after I left you earlier, thinking it would be nice for us to have a run around the countryside before we went to dinner.'

'A car. What a good idea.' Ramon would never find her, she thought, sagging with relief as she got into the passenger seat and leant back against the upholstery. Denis slid in beside her and with a crunch of rubber on gravel they were moving off the car park and on to the road leading to the forest of El Yunque.

Chapter Nine

Denis drove in silence until he reached a place where he could draw right off the road and tuck the car away out of sight. They were in the forest or, rather, on the edge, and the sun was beginning to drop, its long slanting rays picking out the raindrops on the foliage which almost surrounded the car. He turned to Paula, his anxious eyes scanning her face. She had had time to regain some of her composure and there was little evidence either of her tears or the violent scene which had been enacted in the office only a few moments before she had managed to escape.

'Tell me all about it,' encouraged Denis soothingly, as if he were speaking to a child. 'You almost looked as if he had used violence on you.'

Her lip quivered and it was a while before she began to speak. She did begin eventually, and continued uninterrupted till the end.

'I've run away,' she said finally, 'but what do I do now?'

He remained silent for a space, his good-natured face thoughtful and anxious.

'If only you could come with me,' he said. 'I wonder if they are taking on new passengers here. They've been taking them on at some of the other islands we've stopped at, so I don't see why you can't get a cabin. We'd have to make haste, though, as the travel agencies will be closing very soon.'

She was shaking her head.

'I can't make a decision that quick, Denis. Besides, all my clothes are at the casa; I could scarcely go on board a cruise ship with nothing but what I'm standing up in. I've no money, either. It's all there, in the house.'

He frowned and gave a deep sigh.

'What are we to do, then?'

'I shall have to go back,' she faltered, a fit of trembling seizing her at the thought of returning to a husband whose temper was bound to be at its height. Even at this moment he must be fuming at her managing to elude him. He would ask her where she had been, and without a doubt she would find herself confessing that she had met Denis and accepted a ride in his car.

'Can you manage to get your clothes and money out without his knowing?'

She shook her head, saying that such a thing was impossible.

'He'll watch my every move from now on,' she predicted in a desolate tone of voice. She turned her head and Denis turned his at the same time. His lips met hers in a long and tender kiss, and their arms came about each other.

'Paula, dear, what are we going to do?'

She gave a sigh, drew away from him and met his anxious gaze hesitantly.

'Denis . . . I know you will think I'm crazy, but—but I can't make up my mind whether I want to leave Ramon or not—'

'Can't make up your mind!' he exclaimed, flabbergasted. 'Paula, what on earth is wrong with you?'

She swallowed the saliva collecting on her tongue.

'I felt at first that I wanted to stay with him and find some way of punishing him, but then, today, I decided it was best to leave him, because he frightened me so much.' She paused and shook her head distractedly. 'Now, though, I can't bear the thought of leaving him.'

'Because you think Rosa will step in?'

She shook her head.

'No. I'm sure he meant it when he said he'd finished with her. He'd never marry Rosa now.'

'Then why can't you bear to leave him?' He looked at her frowningly and she could not answer. 'It's because you love him?'

She caught her underlip between her teeth.

'Yes,' she replied forlornly, 'I expect that is the reason. He asked me to say I'd stay with him, and I did.'

'That was before he treated you so violently, I take it?'

'Yes, it was.'

'Are you willing to be ill-treated, Paula?' he inquired, and there was no mistaking the hint of contempt in his voice.

She coloured at the implication.

'You despise me? You think I am one of those women who like to be subjugated?'

'I can't think what this man has done to you.'
There was a baffled expression on his face.
'Whatever his hold over you, it's unhealthy. He's
totally dominant and that isn't today's trend.
Woman have been fighting subjugation for a
long while and they've gained equality at last.
It's not natural for you to accept domination,
especially from a man who has admitted openly
that he has no love for you. Why, you're returning to the primitive!' he flashed in disgust.

The primitive. . . . When man was master and
woman obeyed his every whim and wish. Was
that to be her life if she decided to stay with
Ramon? Must she bow her will to his? His face
flashed before her, a face carved in a proud and
classic mould, an arrogant face which rarely
softened, its eyes hard as flint, its mouth full-
lipped, sensuous. . . . Her reverie was broken by
Denis winding down his window. The atmosphere vibrated with the high-toned drilling of
cicadas. It had rained recently but now the road
was drying, and had it been earlier in the
afternoon a cloud of steam would have been
rising from it, for this was tropical forest do-
main. A brightly-plumed parrot flitted through
the branches of a tree, screeching as it disappeared into the dense, jungle vegetation.

All was silent; she recalled the day she had
come up here with Ramon; she had been in a
much happier frame of mind then.

'Well,'' Denis said at last, 'have you made up
your mind?'

She looked at him in profile, and knew for sure
that although he was willing to make an attempt
to help her, he was becoming impatient at her
hesitancy, her inability to make up her mind.

'I ought to leave him,' she said.

'That's no answer.'

'In any case, I can't leave him today.'

'That's no answer either.'

'I'm sorry.'

'Paula,' he said turning towards her, 'I don't believe for one moment that you have any intention of leaving him! He's captured you, body and soul, and you're helpless. My God, if that is love, then I hope I never get entangled with it! He'll crucify you!'

'I must have time,' she quivered. 'Leaving one's husband isn't something you can do impulsively.'

'You married him impulsively,' he could not help reminding her, and now a hostile note had crept into his voice. 'I take it you want me to drive you back to town?'

There was the smallest pause before she said apologetically, 'Yes, please, Denis—and—and I'm sorry. . . .'

No answer; he started the engine, selected the gear and jabbed the accelerator. She had never seen Denis angry before, and she found herself saying on a little sigh that was almost a sob, 'Forgive me, Denis. This is something beyond me—I—I've no control over it—I wish I had because I know I'm behaving most irrationally. You see,' she added, aware of a dry, salty taste in her mouth, 'I'm terrified of going home—'

'Then for God's sake, why go?'

'My things, and money—'

'That's not the damned reason and you know it! You just can't keep away from the man, and even if you knew he was going to beat you, you'd still go back!'

Vivid colour swept into her face.

'He'll—he'll n-not do th-that.'

'You don't sound too sure.' He cast a sideways glance, expelling a breath exasperatedly.

'He'll certainly be angry,' she owned, a catch in her voice.

'Married a fortnight and you're terrified of going home! What the hell's wrong with you? I never remember you being so lacking in common sense!' He paused a moment, his anger swiftly evaporating. 'Let me drive you home, and you can collect your money and belongings. Then we'll go straight to the ship and get you a cabin for the rest of the cruise. We'll land in England together and I'll take you home to mother until you sort yourself out.' Taking his foot off the accelerator, he slowed down almost to a stop. 'Does that appeal to you, dear?'

She hesitated; it all sounded so easy, and she would have Denis to lean on. Once again she felt she needed him, and the temptation to take the easiest way out was very great. But against it rose the image of her husband . . . and she knew she needed him too, but in a very different way. In her confusion of mind she saw vaguely the possibility of revenge, but it took no concrete form. Yet undoubtedly to pay him back would afford her a great amount of satisfaction; she loved him but wanted to hurt him. It was all very illogical but human—an eye for an eye. . . .

'No, Denis,' she decided at last. 'I'll go home and—and see how things turn out. If I find life's becoming too difficult, I shall certainly leave Ramon and return to England.'

A pause ensued before Denis put his foot down and the car gained speed. The forest on either side of the road was darkening, with the sun's rays losing strength but gaining colour. The atmosphere was golden, the forest deep and mysterious and Paula wondered just how much of it was still untrodden by man.

'Do you want me to drop you at your door?' Denis's voice lacked expression, but it was by no means cold and Paula, heartened, felt sure she had not lost him altogether.

'No, just along from it, please, Denis.'

'Very well. You'll have to guide me once we enter the old city.'

'We're going to keep in touch?' she asked a little later.

'If that is what you want. But how is it to be done? That husband of yours isn't going to allow you to receive letters from me.'

'I could get a post box,' she suggested.

'That's an idea.'

'You don't blame me too much over all this?' He slanted her a glance.

'I do and I don't. The trouble is I haven't a clue about women in love. Are they all an enigma like you?'

She coloured slightly.

'I suppose I am a puzzle,' she admitted. 'But if it's any consolation, I'm a puzzle to myself, too. I don't know what I want. To go with you and get on the ship—presupposing I could—seems so simple and uncomplicated. I know your mother would have me till I got settled. But on the other hand, I *am* married. Ramon *is* my husband and I know that he would never walk out on me.'

'You don't know any such thing,' argued Denis. 'He's a rake, a womaniser, and in my opinion a man like that rarely changes his way of life. One woman isn't any good to him; he wants change, craves it. It's in the blood of these Latin American types; they're noted for their infidelity.'

Paula gave a sigh.

'If it turns out like that, I can always leave,' she said.

'If you haven't got a houseful of kids!'

'I shan't have that many,' she said, surprising herself by laughing at the idea.

'Even one would be a tie to a girl like you.'

She nodded in agreement and said unthinkingly, 'Ramon said we must raise a family.'

'He said you *must*. The big boss who wants an heir and sees that his wife gives him one!'

'Don't,' pleaded Paula. 'If I choose to stay with Ramon he will naturally expect children to come.'

'Does he strike you as a family man?' Denis's voice was softer but sarcastic.

'I think he could be,' mused Paula. 'I'm sure he'd make a good father, but perhaps an over-stern one.'

Denis said nothing. Paula directed him and soon he was sliding the car to a standstill a few yards from the entrance to the Casa Don Felipe.

'I'd like to have had dinner with you,' he said, turning to her in the darkness of the car. 'But it wouldn't have done for you to go in so late.'

'I intended to,' she reminded him. 'I'd made up my mind to spend the whole day and evening with you.'

'And then face the irate husband? You're not that brave,' he said.

'We'll not lose touch, Denis—promise.'

'I promise.' He gave a little sigh, then took her

in his arms. 'Get your post office box and then send me the number. 'Goodbye, dear. . . .' His mouth came down to meet hers. They kissed long and passionately, Paula's arms creeping up around his neck. In this moment her mind was more confused than ever; she would, with a small amount of persuasion, have abandoned the idea of staying with her husband and gone back to England with Denis. The whole trouble was that she was terrified of meeting Ramon after running out on him the way she had.

'Denis . . . I . . .'

'You still don't know, do you? But the present situation mustn't be allowed to influence you, Paula; we're both emotionally affected and it's hard to see straight. I feel I could persuade you to come with me, and if I were madly in love with you I'd not hesitate. But we've admitted we're not in love, so let us leave it as it is. Go back, and if it doesn't work, then we shall take up where we left off.'

She nodded, then rested her head on his shoulder.

'You've got so much more sense than I,' she quivered. 'This confusion's terrible. I feel that I'd like to be somewhere on my own, away from everything that could influence me. Then I might be able to sort myself out.'

'He attracts you, that's for sure.'

'It's true, and if only he loved me, life would be heaven.'

'For how long?' The scepticism in his tone was strongly pronounced.

'I know I live in a dream world—or, at least, I did.'

'You'll grow out of it,' he declared, suddenly cynical.

She moved, opening the car door.

'I'd better go,' she said.

'Still scared?' The irony in his voice could not escape her.

'I'm afraid so.'

She drew a frown from him.

'I wish I could do something to help.' He slipped from the car and went round to her side. She stood up, close to him and his arms encircled her. She lifted her face for his kiss, then her nerves tingled.

'Is—is there someone about?' she queried, drawing away from him to glance all around, her eyes peering into the mothy darkness.

'I didn't hear anything.' He kissed her lightly, squeezed her hand, and let her go. 'Goodbye—and good luck.'

An automatic 'goodbye' came to her lips and was stopped. In the chaotic turmoil of her mind the word was too final. If things did not work out with Ramon, Denis was her only hope. If Ramon should terrify her tonight to the point where she was driven to running from him again, Denis was the only one to whom she could go for help.

The engine was running; panic seized her and she stepped forward, but the car began to move. Denis gave a flip of his hand then turned his attention to the road. Paula stood there, a lone, forlorn figure in the creamy moonglow filtering the trees as the bright silver ball emerged from behind a veil of cirrus cloud.

Chapter Ten

It seemed that every single light in the house was on as Paula entered through the front door, which, to her surprise, was slightly ajar. This was a relief to her, as she had fully expected to have to ring for the housekeeper to let her in. Adela with her swift perception would already guess something was wrong, for Paula and Ramon invariably arrived home from the office together.

Paula went upstairs silently and entered the bedroom, her heart throbbing so violently against her ribs that she felt physically sick. To her relief Ramon was neither in the big bedroom nor in the one adjoining.

A shower might revive me a little, she thought, and took one, staying under a long while and then towelling herself dry and making liberal use of the talcum powder. She felt better, more composed, but a shock awaited her when, with the bath-sheet wrapped around her and tucked in beneath her armpits, she came from the bathroom into the bedroom. Ramon was there, and she felt he had been there some time, listening to the shower water, and waiting for her to emerge. Her face drained of colour and it seemed that every nerve in her body was out of control.

'I didn't kn-know you were—were there,' she said trembling. 'I've been—er—having a shower.'

'So I see.' His voice was curt, his eyes lingering on her pale, drawn face.

'I'll g-get dressed.' She turned to the wardrobe, clutching the towel even though it was securely fastened. 'Did you w-want to speak to me about s-something?'

'Where have you been?'

'I walked for a while—in Old San Juan.'

'And then?'

'I—' She stopped, the lump in her throat blocking it. She had been going to tell Ramon the truth, but his manner seemed to warn her not to. He was so quiet, so unemotional. It was most unnatural and she suspected that a terrible fury simmered beneath this smooth unfathomable veneer. 'I just kept on walking.' She opened the wardrobe door and took out an evening dress of crisp, lime green net and lace. 'Can I get to those drawers?' He moved aside and she took out dainty underwear to match the dress.

'You kept on walking, did you?' Soft the voice now, but Paula's heart gave a painful jerk as she detected the gutteral note deep within it. *Will he murder me?* she thought, taking the underwear and dress towards the bathroom door. 'Where did you walk to in all that time?'

'Oh—' She gave a careless shrug of her shoulders. 'All over the place—'

'Don't lie!' With the smooth gliding leap of a jungle animal he had covered the distance between them and was towering above her, a scowling menacing figure, his face like thunder. 'You were with a man, in a car. Who was he?'

She stepped back, a move that incensed him for his nostrils flared. Never had she thought to be so intimidated by a man, by a husband to whom she had been married a mere fortnight.

'It was Denis,' she managed, but unsteadily. 'I happened to run into him in Old San Juan. He had hired a car and—and we drove to—to the forest.' She stopped, pressing a hand to her heart because its wild pounding frightened her. She was sure Ramon could hear it—but perhaps not, for his breathing was heavy, escaping with a hissing sound through teeth that were clenched and visible, for his lips were drawn back in the manner of a snarling beast ready to attack.

Why hadn't she seized the opportunity offered by Denis? She would have been safely away now from this dark foreigner who seemed to revel in frightening her, in reducing her bones to jelly.

'He made love to you up there, in the forest?' Again the voice was soft, dangerously so, and the dark eyes bored into her, as if they would look into her very soul.

His words changed everything. She sent him a glance of burning hatred, lifted her chin and said in a voice vibrating with fury, 'You're detestable! How dare you stand there and accuse me of *that*! My God,' she added contemptuously, 'who are you to accuse anyone of misconduct of that kind—profligate that you are! Get out of my way—I'm packing my things and leaving you, tonight!' In her fury she thrust her hands against his chest hoping to take him by surprise and send him off balance, and it seemed at first that she had succeeded, but he regained his balance and with a savage exclamation gripped her hand in an iron-hard fist and brought her against the hard wall of his chest. She struggled, forgetful of the fact that her only covering was the towel.

'Stop struggling!' he commanded, shaking her. 'I saw you kissing him in the car, and then again outside, so all this indignation's lost on me!'

'You were there, spying on us in the car—and then again when we got out?' So it hadn't been imagination when she had thought there was someone near.

'I've been out looking for you—searching everywhere—'

'If you saw us,' she broke in curiously, 'then why didn't you show yourself?'

The dark Spanish eyes became pools of molten lava.

'I couldn't trust myself. I'd have killed him and almost strangled you! You got out of the car and that saved us all!'

God, what violence was he capable of? Looking up into a face lined with evil she could well believe that he meant what he said. And yet it seemed incredible, the suave, aristocratic Spanish gentleman whom she had first met, and been awed by, turning to violence. It was out of all proportion, she suddenly realised. He did not love her, so why the fierce resentment when she had let her old friend kiss her, the friend she had been keeping company with before she left England?

'I wish I could understand you,' she faltered. 'Why should you have bothered to come looking for me anyway? You must have known I'd come back, since all my clothes and money are here.'

He merely stared, a muscle pulsating in his neck, his dark eyes still on fire. His mouth came closer; she braced herself for the pain she expected him to inflict even while she began to struggle. Her chin was gripped in a steel vice, her lips crushed by the savage possession of his. They moved presently, to explore the sensitive nerves of her throat and the lobe of her ear. 'You're mine!' he snarled, 'get that, and keep it in mind because you'll forget it at your cost!' In his fury he lapsed into Spanish as he added, 'If I did what was right, I'd punish you as you deserve for allowing another man to kiss you!' Instead, he crushed her to his chest, his lean brown fingers sliding down inside the towel which was already coming loose. Fire licked her flesh and ripped through her veins, driving the blood to her heart. His tongue probed her mouth, setting every nerve in her body vibrating as its roughness explored, creating turbulence that she admitted was desire. She clung to him, breathing heavily, forgetting everything but the urgency of her need of him. But without a warning he released her and stood away; she gripped the towel as it began to fall and brought it up over her chest. 'You were about to get dressed,' Ramon said, and now he was almost in full control both of his anger and his passion. 'I'll leave you, then.' Without another word he strode to the door and passed through it. Paula, the towel still clutched in her fingers, stared disbelievingly, her mind in turmoil. Why had he left her, without inflicting much punishment at all? She had prepared herself for some sort of retaliation for what she had done. In fact, there was that moment when she had believed she must pack up and leave here tonight. She had visualised taking a taxi to the ship and asking for Denis, then enlisting his help in getting a cabin. Instead, she was able to stay here; she felt safe . . . but frustrated as well, left like this, ignored after the deliberate temptations of her husband had destroyed all her resistance.

Her eyes fell to the garments she had placed ready to put on; she got into them and looked at herself in the mirror. Her eyes were dull, but otherwise she was satisfied with her appearance. It seemed a miracle that what she had been through had left no marks.

Ramon, immaculate in a beige linen suit and white frilled shirt, was in the main saloon when she entered. Their eyes met for a fleeting moment before he lowered his. Paula gasped. He was actually ashamed! It didn't seem possible, but she was sure she had not been mistaken.

He got her a drink, gave it to her and then, after a long and undecided pause he said, 'I thought you said you were leaving.'

She stared, wondering at the cold indifference of his manner.

'Do you want me to go?' she asked. He did not immediately answer and she added, 'It didn't seem just now as if you wanted me to go.'

'I've been thinking since then, and in view of my reason for marrying you, I feel you have the right to make a choice. If you want to leave, then I won't stop you.' He was watching her closely and she turned her face away, aware that the colour was slowly receding from her cheeks. So he didn't care if she left him. Perhaps he was thinking of Rosa, whom he loved, and decided it was illogical to harbour hatred alongside his love for her. He could be happy if he married her, and so he was offering Paula her freedom.

Her first impulse was to say she would leave at once, but two things prevented her making a decision. Firstly, she was by no means sure that, were she to arrive at Denis's ship with her luggage, she would be able to get aboard. Every cabin might be booked, or it could be that new passengers were not being taken aboard in Puerto Rico. And secondly, she knew a fierce resentment at her husband's decision to let her go; it was for his own ends, to make the way clear for a resumption of his relationship with the girl to whom he was once engaged. She, Paula, was his wife and she had certain rights. She would assert them! She would stand between Ramon and his ex-fiancée for just as long as it was possible!

Several days went by, with the strained atmosphere between Paula and her husband increasing all the time. Ramon slept in his own room; he dined with Paula, but rarely spoke to her. He still had her go to the office, but often used the young clerk rather than have Paula go into his private office. Time began to drag; Paula had never been so bored in her life and she began to wonder how much longer she would be able to tolerate the loneliness. Her love for Ramon was as strong as ever, his magnetism still effective, even though he never so much as kissed her. His goodnights were short and brusque, as were his morning greetings at the breakfast table. She suspected it was a wearing down process calculated to drive her to make the decision to leave him. She found her temper rising whenever he ignored her altogether, and she began to snap at him when he did speak to her. One evening after dinner he spoke seriously to her, saying that this situation could not continue much longer.

'It's uncomfortable for us both,' he added broodingly. 'Why don't you go? I've said I won't do anything to stop you.'

Paula's eyes blazed.

'I shall stay as long as I like,' she flashed. 'This is *my* home and I don't intend to leave it until it suits me!'

'What good is it doing for you to stay?'

'If my presence here annoys and inconveniences you, then staying does me a whole world of good!'

'Revenge, eh?' His voice was low and bitter.

'*You* enjoyed it, so why shouldn't *I*?'

'Two wrongs never add up to a right, Paula.'

She flashed him a curious glance.

'You sound as if you regret what you did to me,' she said, scanning his features closely, looking for any sign of contrition or remorse. But his face was the set mask she had become used to of late and she read nothing from it.

'Are you going to leave?' he asked, ignoring her comments. 'I'll make you an allowance—a large one—'

'Keep your money,' she broke in contemptuously. 'Spend it on the long string of mistresses who'll be passing through your life for the next twenty or thirty years!'

His dark brows lifted a fraction. Paula suspected he was both angry and surprised that she could speak like that. However, he bypassed this just as he had bypassed her earlier comments.

'I think you'll agree, Paula, that we should seriously discuss separation, and a settlement for you. This life is not only unbearable but degrading. It's false and it's boring, for us both.' He looked at her with a directness meant to add force to his words and it did. Mentally she agreed with all he had said, and she accepted that the life they were leading could not continue indefinitely. Yet she was still reluctant to leave, to walk out and make it easy for Ramon to pick up where he left off before they met and married. She had told Denis that she was sure he would never marry Rosa, but now she was by no means sure. Jealousy flared within her, searing her mind, tearing at her heartstrings.

'I shall not leave,' she declared, her chin high, her eyes wide and bright with determination. 'You married me and you will have to put up with me! I'm here to stay, Ramon! You're not casting me off as if I was one of your women of the moment!'

'How long do you suppose you can live this kind of life?' he queried. They were in the saloon and he had a glass in his hand. His eyes left his wife's face to focus on the liquid in the glass; he seemed to become absorbed in the sparks of light reflecting through it and on to his fingers. Paula, leaning back in her chair, watched him in silence for a while, wishing she could read his thoughts, wishing she could understand the workings of his mind. He glanced at her inquiringly and she answered his question.

'I do admit that it can't go on forever, but I mean it to continue for a long while yet. I'm not usually a vindictive person, but I intend to make you pay for what you did to me. I shall be around to annoy you by my presence, Ramon, so you might as well become resigned.'

'It's obvious that you are not in love with Denis?'

'You know very well that I'm not.' *Surely he knew she was still in love with* him, she thought, puzzled by his words. Or had he assumed that her love was dead, killed by the knife-sharp pangs of disillusionment? Yes, she realised all at once, he did believe that her love was dead. Well, that at least made her feel much better, for nothing had been more humiliating in all this than the constant awareness that her husband knew she loved him. 'I could be one day, though,' she was urged to say. 'He and I are keeping in touch, and if ever I do decide to leave you and have a divorce, then he and I will marry.'

Ramon was frowning heavily, and looked at her in disbelief.

'You're not in love and yet you'd marry him?' His expression changed to one of suspicion. 'You're lying, Paula. A situation like the one you're describing could not possibly exist.' He paused a moment, the glass to his lips, his dark gaze meeting hers from above the rim. He seemed to be hesitant, going over words mentally to see if they were what he wanted to say. She saw his expression change to one of resolution before he said, 'If you choose to stay, then you

must resign yourself to my living my own life—
the life I lived before I married you.' Turning
abruptly, he went over to the cabinet and poured
himself another drink. Paula put a hand to her
heart, because the pain was excruciating, the
wild throbbing frightened her. He meant to live
the profligate life, going out with women, staying out all night—perhaps bringing them home
and sleeping with them here. . . .

She said, a tremor in her voice which she
hoped he would not notice, 'You mean—you'll
have—have women coming here?'

'It's possible,' he replied indifferently.

'You'd humiliate me in that way?' There was a
distinct break in her voice now which she could
not possibly disguise.

'If you choose to stay then it will be your own
fault if you're humiliated,' he said over his
shoulder. 'Think about it carefully, Paula, before
you take this adamant stand which you've admitted stems from the desire for revenge and
nothing else. It will be better all around if you
leave me now.'

She stared dumbly at his broad back, the pain
of her heart reflected in her face, in the sudden
prominence of cheekbones robbed of colour and
over which the transparent skin seemed to have
become more tightly stretched.

'If I stay, you will come and go as you
please . . . ?' Her voice trailed away to silence as
she wondered why she was speaking like this
when she had been told what Ramon intended to
do.

'Of course. My life is my own.' He was tilting a
bottle of brandy, pouring the amber liquid into
his glass. Paula, watching him, found herself

being surprised when he did not fill the glass. He seemed in the mood to take more than was good for him. But he was moderate in his drinking habits, she had noticed, and had only taken more than usual if he had been in one of his brooding, distant moods.

'Supposing I do the same?' The suggestion came unbidden; she had no intention of doing the same.

He seemed to stiffen in every muscle, and the hand holding the glass tightened so that Paula expected to see the fragile crystal break and fall to the floor, spilling the brandy on to the carpet.

'I would not permit that,' he said tautly.

'Oh, and why? If you are unfaithful to me, then I have every right to do the same to you.'

He turned and she flinched at the harshness of his face.

'So we get back to what our parents did.'

'It was your suggestion. Fortunately there are no children to suffer as a result of our actions.' How calm she sounded! It was a miracle, considering the way her heart was beating overrate, her nerves pulsing, out of control.

'I have said I will not permit you to have other men,' he told her inexorably, his dark eyes fixing hers in a warning look. 'Flout my wishes and I shall punish you.'

High colour leapt to her cheeks as anger flared.

'I shall do exactly as you do!' she threatened, her small fists clenched on her lap. 'If you have other women, then I shall have other men—' She broke off, trembling as he came purposefully towards her. 'Touch me and I'll scream for Adela!' she warned, white to the lips. 'You've used violence on me for the last time,' she managed, but in a voice that quivered, lacking conviction.

He stopped, eyes glinting, tiny threads of crimson creeping along the sides of his mouth, the evidence of fury held in check.

'I can force you to leave me,' he assured her after a long, intense silence. 'In England the law might allow a wife to stay in her husband's house, but here our laws are different. As long as I compensate you adequately, I can turn you out of my home.'

She stared at him with growing suspicion. His face was impassive and even as she fixed his eyes he turned from her, to take up the brandy glass he had placed on a table.

'I don't believe you,' she murmured. 'You're just saying that because you want to be rid of me.'

'It's for the best.'

'That happens to be your opinion.'

'And yours, if you were honest.'

She fell silent, her mind in total confusion. She ought to leave, to accept the compensation he would offer and get herself established in England again. She felt sure he would give her more than enough for her to get a flat and furnish it, and even to carry on without a job if she had difficulty in getting one. Yes, it was the sensible thing to do, she decided, all her other resolutions going by the board. Revenge was all right, but if it hurt her more than it hurt him it was stupid to indulge in it.

'I'll go then,' she told him dully. 'If—if you can arrange everything f-for me—the flight and—and anything else. . . .' Tears stung her eyes but

she bravely held them back. He was not going to
see just how much she was hurt. He believed
her love was dead and she had no intention of
doing anything that might give him cause to
suspect he was mistaken. 'I'll go to bed—
goodnight. . . .' Unsteadily she rose from the
chair, her head averted because she dared not
let him see her expression and what it
revealed—the pain and hopelessness, the dull
resignation, the misery.

'Goodnight, Paula.' His voice was taut, with
an odd, unfathomable inflection in its depths.
'Sleep well. And do not worry about the future.
You will be well taken care of. . . .' His voice
trailed and she turned wonderingly, forgetful
that she did not want him to see what was in her
eyes. He was going slowly towards the window,
so she saw only his back. She closed her eyes
tightly against the ready tears that were quickly
filling them.

'Goodnight,' she murmured huskily and left
the room, closing the door softly behind her.

For the next couple of days Ramon was absent
both from home and office. He was going to
Haiti, he had told Adela, but Paula felt sure he
was still in San Juan, but he was keeping out of
her way until the day of her departure which
was on the Tuesday following her decision to
leave. It arrived and she awoke with a sensation
of having a ton weight resting on her body,
crushing it, numbing all feeling and thought.
She rose and moved mechanically to the window. The scene which had so delighted her on
her arrival in the old city was dull and uninter-
esting in the atmosphere of low, ominous cloud

that hung over it. The sun shut out. . . . How fitting for the day when she was to leave it all. Turning, dry-eyed and without mental or physical awareness of anything much at all, she showered and dressed, remembering to include in her hand luggage some clothes which would be serviceable for the colder climate of England. All was ready when Ramon appeared; she heard his car scrape to a halt on the gravel and automatically looked down, her heart contracting as he came from the car with lithe and easy steps that made it seem he was in a nonchalant, satisfied frame of mind. He had phoned her late last night to say he would be there to drive her to the airport. She heard his voice as he spoke to Adela and she wondered what explanation he meant to give. She was soon to learn that he had merely said she was paying a visit to relatives in England and would be away for a few weeks.

'I can say, later, that you decided to stay,' he told Paula as they watched her luggage being loaded into the back of the car. 'I'll say that you couldn't settle here and so we have agreed on a divorce.' He paused a moment, but Paula could not speak for the agonising blockage in her throat. This was so final, the loading of her possessions into the car in readiness for its journey to the airport. 'I shall arrange an immediate transfer of money to the bank you mentioned,' he promised. 'You will have quite a large sum to draw on.'

She did not thank him, and when presently they were driving to the airport it was a silent journey, each being occupied by their own thoughts. He saw her suitcases checked in, made sure she had her documents with her and

then they stood facing one another in that final moment before saying goodbye. His eyes
were dark and brooding, hers filmed with tears,
and dark with unhappiness. A tense unfathomable silence hung between them like an insur-
mountable barrier. She felt his hand take hers,
its warmth and strength sending pulsations
through her body. He said goodbye and then
without another word he was striding away, out
of her life without a backward glance.

She made her way to the lounge, her first class
ticket clutched tightly in her fingers and in her
other hand the rather heavy piece of luggage she
was taking into the cabin. People were milling
about, chatting together, laughing. . . . She felt
lost and alone, with a dry, choking sensation in
her throat, and she wished that she could die.

The plane was late and it was dark before
Paula was at last on board, her seat belt fastened. The roar of the engines increased and as
she felt the pressure on her back Paula realised
they were taking off. She glanced through the
window, wondering where in the blackness
beyond the airfield her husband was. Could he
be sparing a thought for her—? Her unhappy
musings stopped abruptly as her heart jerked
right up into her mouth on the sudden violent
lurching of the aircraft. Someone screamed; the
tip of the wing hit the ground and on the instant
sparks shot into the air. The blazing wingtip
came up again but the next moment there was a
shuddering, grinding noise and the plane spun
into a ground loop and slowed to a stop. Paula,
her heart thudding against her ribs, wanted
nothing more than to rise from her seat, but
controlled the impulse as the stewards and

stewardesses began opening the doors and escape hatches. The next few minutes were like
an eternity before it was Paula's turn to be
guided to the shoot and told to slide down it. The
fire was on the other side of the aircraft and the
doors on that side were still firmly closed. Fire
engines screamed along the runway, their lights
trained on the airplane. From another direction
a fleet of ambulances was approaching the
crippled aircraft.

Dazed, but conscious that she was safe, Paula
found herself back in the lounge. She heard
someone say that the accident had been caused
by a burst tire; she also heard that no one had
been hurt.

'Paula!' The voice calling her name seemed to
come from a long way off and yet it was loud and
clear. Her heart turned a somersault; she twisted her head to look into the grey, haggard face of
her husband.

'Ramon,' she quivered disbelievingly, 'how—
what—?'

'I stayed in the observation lounge to see your
plane leave—' He stopped, and at the ghastly
colour that was spreading over his face Paula
half-expected him to be sick. Nerves were pulsating in his throat and in his left cheek; perspiration was oozing from his forehead and upper
lip. 'I saw the sparks, then the fire—' His voice
faltered again and Paula, her eyes widening to
their fullest extent, felt her pulses race . . . and
this time it was something very different from
fear that was the cause. . . .

It was half an hour later that she heard herself
say, 'I never thought I'd be grateful for a plane

accident, Ramon. Oh, but why didn't you tell me you loved me before?'

'I intended to, but then things began to happen. Your friend Denis appeared and I saw you in his arms—' His words came to a stop when Paula put her fingers to his lips. They were on the balcony of the Casa Don Felipe, their arms about each other, their eyes staring over the lights of the city to where the moon hung low over the massive ramparts of the citadel. Ramon had brought her home where, he said, she would stay. He had explained much in the short drive from the airport to the house, and Paula learned that after seeing her with Denis in the car he had decided it was too late to confess that he loved her. He had killed her love by his treatment of her and although at first he had no intention of letting her go, he soon became filled with shame and remorse and felt that the only recompense he could make was to give her her freedom and a large settlement that would ensure her comfort and security for the rest of her life. 'It was sheer hell, letting you go,' he admitted. 'And you didn't make it any easier by saying you weren't leaving until you were ready. I knew I couldn't live in the same house and resist making love to you, and it did seem that, as you weren't in love with me—'

'But I was,' she could not help interrupting, going up on tiptoe to kiss him.

'I know that now, darling, but at the time I didn't, remember? And so it seemed that I would be taking you by force, and each time it happened you'd hate me a little more—'

'You really think so?' she broke in, curling her

fingers along his nape and up into his thick dark hair.

'Sweetheart,' he chided softly, 'if you didn't keep interrupting I could finish my story and we could concentrate on more pleasurable pursuits.' He was laughing with his eyes. He bent his head and his lips met hers in a long and passionate kiss. 'As I was saying, you didn't make things easier by your decision to stay. So I had to make threats about living the old life—'

'It was cruel,' she accused petulantly, like a fractious child, and her husband gave her a little shake as punishment.

'I had to be cruel to be kind,' he went on after the interruption. 'I was doing what was the best for you—'

'What you *thought* was the best for me,' she corrected and received another shake for interrupting.

'I felt I owed you such a lot—'

'You could have repaid it by saying you loved me.'

'Paula,' said her husband in a dangerously soft voice, 'do you stop interrupting or do I put you over my knee and spank you so hard you'll not sit down for a week?'

She buried her face in his shoulder, vitally aware of his body warmth against her cheek.

'I won't interrupt again,' she promised, but she did add that it was a very long story and she had guessed a great deal from what he had already told her.

'Well, I intend to finish it,' he said. 'The hardest thing I have ever done in my life was to go away for those days before you were due to leave. Yet I had to, darling, for otherwise I'd have taken you by force. Then came another hard part: the taking you to the airport—'

'But why didn't you give me some hint of how you felt?' she broke in protestingly. 'I had no clue that you cared, Ramon—not one from the very beginning. And you did admit that you loved Rosa, you know,' she added as the thought occurred to her.

'At the time I genuinely believed I was telling the truth. Yet even then I was attracted by you, by your beauty, dearest, and your charming naïveté, your sincerity— Oh, so many endearing traits! Let me kiss you before I say any more!' And, suiting his action to his words, he crushed her eager body to him and kissed her with all the arrogant possessiveness of his Spanish ancestors.

She was breathless and laughing when at last he released her. She stared up into his face and thought what a difference there was from so short a time ago when he came to her in the airport lounge. He had convinced himself she had been killed, he had confessed on the way home. His life would not have been worth living, he admitted, for he would have blamed himself for her death, simply because, but for his treatment of her, she would not have been aboard the airplane.

She had smiled then, and told him her love had never waned, and all she had ever wanted was to have his love in return.

Yes, she mused as she stood close to him on the balcony, much had been cleared up during the short drive home, and now the rest was explained—or most of it. Anything else could wait, they both seemed to decide as they pressed their hungry bodies together, their lips meeting, their arms tight about each other.

'I love you, my dear, dear husband,' whispered Paula simply. 'Be with me always . . . always. . . .' She leant away, her eyes adoring.

'Always and forever,' was his fervent promise before, sweeping her passionately into his arms again, he crushed her lips beneath his own in a kiss that was as primitive as it was tender, as arrogantly possessive as it was reverent. 'Always and forever, my dearly beloved wife.'

Silhouette Romance

ROMANCE THE WAY
IT USED TO BE...
AND COULD BE AGAIN

Contemporary romances for today's women

Each month, six very special love stories will be yours from SILHOUETTE. Look for them wherever books are sold or order now from the coupon below.

___#14 RED, RED ROSE Tess Oliver $1.50 (57014-5)
___#15 SEA GYPSY Fern Michaels $1.50 (57015-3)
___#16 SECOND TOMORROW Anne Hampson
$1.50 (57016-1)
___#17 TORMENTING FLAME Nancy John
$1.50 (57017-X)
___#18 THE LION'S SHADOW Elizabeth Hunter
$1.50 (57018-8)
___#19 THE HEART NEVER FORGETS Carolyn Thornton
$1.50 (57019-6)
___#20 ISLAND DESTINY Paula Fulford
$1.50 (57020-X)
___#21 SPRING FIRES Leigh Richards $1.50 (57021-8)
___#22 MEXICAN NIGHTS Jeanne Stephens
$1.50 (57022-6)
___#23 BEWITCHING GRACE Paula Edwards
$1.50 (57023-4)
___#24 SUMMER STORM Letitia Healy $1.50 (57024-2)
___#25 SHADOW OF LOVE Sondra Stanford
$1.50 (57025-0)
___#26 INNOCENT FIRE Brooke Hastings
$1.50 (57026-9)
___#27 THE DAWN STEALS SOFTLY Anne Hampson
$1.50 (57027-7)

SILHOUETTE BOOKS, Department SB/1

1230 Avenue of the Americas, New York, N.Y. 10020

Please send me the books I have checked above. I am enclosing $_____
(please add 50¢ to cover postage and handling for each order, N.Y.S. and N.Y.C.
residents please add appropriate sales tax). Send check or money order—no
cash or C.O.D.s please. Allow up to six weeks for delivery.

NAME_____

ADDRESS_____

CITY_____ STATE/ZIP_____

SB/1-6/80